"D

Her eyes widening at the sound of Matt's deep voice, she jerked around. No, he most definitely did not look like someone who politely obeyed anyone's beck and call. Even with a smile curving his chiseled mouth, the sheer, masculine power betrayed in his careless stance made it clear that he only took orders when he had to. He was much more apt to give them.

She stepped back, consciously fighting the urge to tighten her robe. It didn't make the slightest bit of sense. She'd opened the door to what she'd thought would be a perfect stranger, and her state of dress, or undress, hadn't even occurred to her. Now, seeing Matt standing there, all she could think about was how much her skimpy attire exposed.

Dear Reader:

Series and Spin-offs! Connecting characters and intriguing interconnections to make your head whirl.

In Joan Hohl's successful trilogy for Silhouette Desire—*Texas Gold* (7/86), *California Copper* (10/86), *Nevada Silver* (1/87)—Joan created a cast of characters that just wouldn't quit. You figure out how *Lady Ice* (5/87) connects. And in August, "J.B." demanded his own story—*One Tough Hombre*. In *Falcon's Flight*, coming in November, you'll learn *all* about . . .?

Annette Broadrick's *Return to Yesterday* (6/87) introduced Adam St. Clair. This August *Adam's Story* tells about the woman who saves his life—and teaches him a thing or two about love!

The six Branigan brothers appeared in Leslie Davis Guccione's *Bittersweet Harvest* (10/86) and *Still Waters* (5/87). September brings *Something in Common*, where the eldest of the strapping Irishmen finds love in unexpected places.

Midnight Rambler by Linda Barlow is in October—a special Halloween surprise, and totally unconnected to anything.

Keep an eye out for other Silhouette Desire favorites—Diana Palmer, Dixie Browning, Ann Major and Elizabeth Lowell, to name a few. You never know when secondary characters will insist on their own story. . . .

All the best,

Isabel Swift
Senior Editor & Editorial Coordinator
Silhouette Books

CHRISTINE FLYNN
Meet Me at Midnight

Silhouette Desire

Published by Silhouette Books New York

America's Publisher of Contemporary Romance

SILHOUETTE BOOKS
300 East 42nd St., New York, N.Y. 10017

ISBN: 0-373-05377-0

First Silhouette Books printing September 1987

America's Publisher of Contemporary Romance

Printed in the U.S.A.

CHRISTINE FLYNN

admits to two obsessions: reading and writing, and three "serious" preoccupations: gourmet cooking, her family (she has a daughter, and a husband she unabashedly describes as the sexiest best friend a girl could ever have) and travel. She has tried everything from racing cars to modeling before settling into what she loves best—turning her daydreams into romance novels.

To my editor, Lucia Macro, with thanks.

One

Eden Michaels pulled the wide strap of her travel bag higher on her shoulder, ducking her head as she hurried past the open office door. She wasn't trying to avoid Harry—not him in particular, anyway. It was just that she was due at Security in eleven minutes and if she didn't leave right now, she'd never make it to the other side of the State Department building in time. The last thing she wanted to do was be late. After all, there was no sense getting off on the wrong foot with the men she'd be spending the next month with—even if she did think that whoever called this meeting was nuts for doing it less than an hour before they were all due at the airport.

"Hold it, Eden!"

For a split second she seriously considered ignoring Harry's sharp command. Then, her tawny, shoulder-length hair flying, she swung around to retrace her steps.

Translating her mental Damn!, to a verbal *"Zut!"* when a few resettling strands caught in her dark lashes, she raised her hand to pull them free. The task was impaired somewhat by the way she had her briefcase sandwiched between her arm and her side.

"I heard that." Harry Winston, the beleaguered deputy under secretary for the Bureau of Cultural Affairs, leaned back in his tufted wing chair, his slight frame threatening to tip it right through the window behind him. Grabbing a file from the stack on the windowsill, he muttered, "Your accent's off," as his shifting weight sprang the chair forward again.

Despite her impatience, Eden gave him an elfin smile. There was nothing wrong with her accent and Harry knew it. Her French was excellent, as was her Russian, Spanish, Italian and Portuguese. It was her German that was still a little shaky.

"Did you need something, Harry? I've got to meet with the security people and I'm really running behind."

"That meeting's just a formality. They had to assign a new team head, and he wants to meet you before you all leave. That can wait." He then announced, "Barbara's not back yet, so I want to make sure we've covered everything."

As always, Eden's dusky green eyes betrayed whatever she was feeling at the moment. At this particular moment, it was excitement dampened by her desire that he get on with it. She was eager to get on to her new assignment and couldn't imagine what he'd have to say that he hadn't said already—in triplicate.

"You're going to call me as soon as Dubikov and his people get in tonight?"

Seeing him peer over the top of his rimless glasses, Eden nodded.

"Fine. Now, let's see." Talking more to himself than to her, he sorted through the thick stack of papers. "Security has okayed the arrangements at all the hotels. You're at the St. Clair in Boston until Sunday, then... Oh, good," he continued when something else in the file caught his attention. "Barbara's taken care of the limousine problem in Seattle. Ah, here we go." The furrows in his brow eased considerably when he found the scrap of paper he was looking for. "The conductor of the Boston Symphony won't be at the hotel until noon. He'll meet with Dubikov there for lunch, then you're to..."

While Harry ran down his latest list of notes for the renowned Russian violinist's four-week concert tour, it was easy for Eden to see why her boss was going bald. The man fretted constantly. He'd already told her everything she needed to know. All he was doing now was repeating himself.

Eden knew that a tour of this type wasn't put together overnight, and she certainly appreciated the monumental effort that had gone into it. There came a time, however, when details started getting in the way of the purpose. Harry's insistence that everything be gone over umpteen times was causing him to overlook one very important point. If he didn't let her leave in the next minute, she'd not only upset the security team by being late, but there would be no one to meet Mr. Dubikov's plane.

She was about to mention that when Harry finally glanced up. "And remember, Under Secretary Thompson wants to make sure you keep that first press conference at the airport short. Dubikov and his people are going to be tired and we don't want them thinking the American press are a bunch of vultures."

Refraining from comment on his last remark, she surreptitiously eyed her watch. Four minutes. "Since I'm the interpreter, they'll have to stop asking questions when I stop translating them. Don't worry, Harry, everything's going to be fine."

With a prayerful "I certainly hope so," he stabbed at the blinking light on his phone. Glancing back up, he frowned. "I know you're looking forward to this, but I really wish you wouldn't look quite so enthusiastic. It makes me nervous."

Backing out the door, she ruined her dutiful "Yes, sir" with a brilliant smile—and promptly bumped into Barbara Yu.

Her quick apology was met with a laughing "It's okay" from the slightly stunning Eurasian woman who'd bent to retrieve the briefcase Eden had dropped. "I was hoping I'd run into you before you left."

"Cute, Barb."

"I thought so." The corners of her exotic brown eyes turning up with her grin, Barbara nudged Eden's arm. "Come on. I know you're in a hurry, so we can talk on the way to the elevator. Great suit."

Hurrying down the hall, Eden glanced at the soft cream-colored wool of her slim skirt then back to the extraordinarily efficient bureau secretary. "Thanks. Mom sent it to me from England."

"You can get some great stuff in Europe."

"I know. I picked up this blouse in Rome for next to nothing."

"Raw silk never costs next to nothing, Eden." Turning around after she punched the elevator button, Barb crossed her arms over her outrageously expensive red silk shirt-waist. Married to a very successful attorney, she could afford to pay designer prices. Eden, while she had the same excellent taste, rarely bought anything unless it was on sale. "You all set?"

Anxiously eyeing the indicator light above the metal doors, Eden sighed. "Yeah. I just wish Harry thought so. If I were the paranoid type, I'd swear he thinks I can't remember a thing."

"Nonsense. He's forgotten all about that mix-up with the exchange students from Brazil. Besides, your main responsibility is communications. I'm the one who'll get the flak if any of my arrangements don't work out." The soft ping of the bell drew Barb's attention to the opening doors. Holding the closest one back, she stepped aside for Eden to pass. "Listen, Eden, I don't want to sound like Harry, but—"

"I know," Eden cut in. "If I run into any snags, I'll let you know right away and you'll take care of it. If something comes up and I can't reach the office, the person in charge of security has the final word. I'm to defer to him in every instance."

"You sound like you memorized that memo."

Grinning, Eden wriggled her fingers as the doors began to close. "I think I did. Talk to you soon."

"Call me if you need anything," she heard Barb say through the narrowing gap. "Anything!"

Still smiling to herself, Eden leaned against the wall of the slowly descending, and surprisingly empty, cubicle. Barb was more than just a co-worker. In the five months Eden had known her, she'd become a terrific friend. Who else but a friend would sit quietly sipping wine while you rattled on about how excited you were about an assignment? Especially while you were packing and cleaning all the stuff capable of turning green and fuzzy out of your refrigerator?

In spite of Harry's request that she curb her enthusiasm, Eden couldn't have hidden her anticipation if she'd tried. Not only was she finally getting to travel again, but in less than five hours, she was actually going to meet Nikolai

Dubikov. First, though, she and the security team assigned as his escort had to be at National Airport in time to catch the five-forty shuttle to Boston. Dubikov's flight was due in at Logan International at nine.

No, she corrected, as the doors whooshed open. *First*, she had to attend this ridiculous meeting. Why couldn't she just introduce herself to the new guy when everyone met outside at the cab? There would be plenty of time for that sort of thing on the way to the airport.

Working her way through the maze of halls, she came up with the only plausible answer to that question. This new head security person obviously liked things to be done properly. Which, she supposed, was fine. She had no objection to following proper procedure. It was just that her intentions didn't always coincide with her actions.

A small sigh of relief seemed in order when she reached the conference room. Cooling her heels at the door, Eden could see she wasn't the only one who'd been delayed. Of the three agents she'd accompany on this assignment, only one was in the room. The one she hadn't met. He was standing at the window with his back to her.

Preparing to enter, both her step and her smile of greeting faltered. She wasn't sure what it was exactly, but something about him seemed vaguely familiar.

It wasn't his size, though there was certainly nothing wrong with the way his fairly average six feet or so were put together. Since his suit jacket was presently being worn by one of the chairs at the long, mahogany table, it was easy enough to see that the muscles beneath his white shirt and neatly tapering vest were quite solid. The other half of him wasn't bad, either, Eden thought. With his hands jammed into the pockets of his superbly tailored charcoal slacks, the fabric stretched over his . . .

. . . Billfold, she mentally supplied and jerked her eyes up again. It hadn't been the boldness of her perusal so much as his slight movement that demanded her attempt at identification to return to his head.

At first, she'd thought his hair was black, but it was only the contrast of silver threaded through the rich, deep brown that gave that impression. There was no mistaking that gray for age, though. There was confidence in his stance, an air of raw masculinity that made her think he'd earned that silver through experience.

He turned his head slightly. Catching a glimpse of his strong jaw, she saw his broad shoulders rise as he took a deep breath. "Close the door, Eden. There are a couple of things about this tour I want to talk to you about before the others get here."

Matt Killian. Before he'd even turned around, she knew who he was from the sound of his deep, smoky voice. There were certain things about a person, even one you barely knew, that you just didn't forget.

Matt didn't have the satisfaction of seeing the swift stab of consternation momentarily cloud Eden's expression. It passed so quickly she was barely aware of it herself. More than anything, she simply felt surprise at seeing him here.

Letting only her astonishment show, she did as he'd requested—rather, instructed—and stepped into the spacious room. Matt had once been part of the unobtrusive, but ever present, security detail at the embassy in Italy. Her own assignment there had come to a premature end six months ago. "I haven't seen you in ages, Matt. How've you been?"

It was Matt's turn to be surprised. The least he'd expected from her was a little defensiveness or, possibly, embarrassment. The soft gray-green eyes smiling at him held nothing but pleasure, though. Genuine pleasure, at that.

"Ah, I've been fine." I guess, he added to himself, not at all certain why he felt as if he'd lost ground somehow. He'd been priming himself for this meeting all day and it was a little annoying to find that Eden wasn't acting the way he had expected her to.

Crossing to him, she slipped the strap of her bag from her shoulder. Her bag hit the floor with a thud. "When did you get back?"

"Day before yesterday. Look—"

"And they've already reassigned you? To this tour?"

"I asked for it." Literally, he couldn't help but think. The next time he volunteered to fill in for someone, he'd find out who he'd be working with before committing himself. "McDonald broke his ankle."

"How'd he do that?"

"Jogging."

"Jogging?"

"He hit a pothole."

Frowning, Eden quietly studied Matt's very attractive face. She'd watched more than one diplomat's wife do a double take when he walked into a room. She'd had to look twice herself when she'd first seen him. "That's too bad. You really look tired."

Exhausted is more like it, he thought, wondering at her perception. Jet lag and spending two nights trying to sleep on a too-hard mattress had all but guaranteed the haggard look that had greeted him in the mirror this morning. He wished his sister would get rid of that orthopedic torture-rack in her guest room.

"Gone wading lately?" he drawled, attempting to return the conversation to its proper track.

"Not since Rome." Eyes twinkling, she absently tossed her briefcase onto the conference table. "By the way, I never did get a chance to thank you for the use of your jacket. You did get it back, didn't you?''

"I did," he muttered, sensing his train of thought derailing as the mental picture she'd just conjured sprang back into his mind. "You didn't need to have it cleaned."

"It was the least I could do. You probably prevented me from catching pneumonia. As it was, Eleanor Snow came down with a cold."

Matt let out a slow, steadying breath. The last time he'd seen Eden, she'd been pulled, dripping wet, from Trevi fountain by an embassy guard. Somehow, she and half a dozen other guests from Ambassador Snow's party had wound up going for a midnight swim, and between all the onlookers who'd joined them and the local police trying to calm the chaos, Matt had lost track of his charge—the ambassador's wife.

He'd almost forgotten about that minor breach of security. But he'd never quite been able to forget the laughter he'd seen in Eden's eyes just before he'd started yelling at her—or the way her damp, plunging evening gown had clung to every curve of her slender body.

Exhaustion, he reminded himself. That had to be the reason he kept getting sidetracked. Scowling, he pulled his glance from the contours hidden beneath her fashionably loose jacket. He'd get to the point of this conversation no matter how much she tried to divert him.

"Look, Eden, I don't mean to sound like you don't know what you're doing, but I don't want anything happening that's not on Harry Winston's schedule. We've got twenty-two concerts to cover in eleven different cities. That means my men and I have to get Dubikov, his manager and two bodyguards through airports, into and out of hotels, and escort them to rehearsals. There's also press conferences, receptions and a lecture in Philadelphia." Aware of her mildly indulgent expression as he reiterated what had already been drilled into her, he didn't bother mentioning the various city tours also on Mr. Winston's agenda. Instead, he aimed right for the heart of the matter. "I expect protocol to be observed in every instance."

Her shoulders lifted in a rather elegant shrug. "No problem. Anything else?"

No problem, Matt repeated to himself. She stood there as calm as you please and said, "No problem." The woman clearly didn't appreciate his anxiety. "What do you know about Dubikov?"

A lot more than I do about you, she thought, immediately wondering where that incongruous thought had come from. "That depends on what you mean. I've followed his career ever since I studied his technique in school—"

"That was in France."

"Right. At l'École de Musique. How'd you know that?"

"I read your dossier." Hands shoved in his pockets, he watched her intently. "What else? Do you know anything about him personally?"

He'd read her dossier? "Why?"

"Because it's important to me. I also read the notes from the briefings you attended, but I don't know how much you know about him."

Her quiet "Oh" held the tiniest hint of disappointment. For a second there, she thought he'd been talking about her. "I'm sure your bureau has more personal background on him than it sent over to us. We get what their Ministry of Culture provides. The Soviets are pretty stingy with information about their artists, unless it's something that promotes their talent." It was easy enough to recall the sketchy information she'd pieced together. But in the interest of time, she didn't elaborate or embellish as she often had a tendency to do. "He's apparently never been married and his parents are retired. I have no idea from what, though. That part of his official biography was pretty vague. It didn't mention any siblings, and I've never heard of any. He lives among the elite and is regarded as something of a national monument by his government. That's about it," she started to conclude, then couldn't resist adding, "except that his love of music is surpassed only by his love of women. His government sort of tolerates that, I suppose, but they certainly don't publicize it."

Matt was quite satisfied with her concise account of information about Dubikov. Security handed out information only on a strictly Need to Know basis. Eden's level of security clearance was such that she hadn't been informed of the potential problems the violinist's visit posed.

Since the more intimate details of Dubikov's family history hadn't been shared with Eden, she didn't know that one long-forgotten member of that family had parted company with his country. The department didn't want to jeopardize any future cultural exchanges by having Nikolai Dubikov follow the course his brother had taken thirty years ago. Then, aside from the risk of a potential defection, something Matt had been ordered not to allow, there was the possibility that certain fanatical groups might create some kind of trouble.

Those problems weren't what concerned Matt now, though. The reason for his considered silence was, as Eden had just mentioned, Dubikov's reputation. The musician's roving eye presented an entirely different sort of headache.

"They don't want any publicity about that and neither do we. That's why I want you to do your job, but otherwise stay clear of him."

"What do you mean?"

"I mean you're not to let him get you alone. Not," he continued, matching her frown, "that there's much chance of that happening. You know as well as I do that the people coming with him aren't just along for the ride. They're going to do their best to make sure he doesn't do anything that might embarrass his country. That includes any unnecessary familiarity with members of his host escort. Female members in particular."

It was as she stood there, her bottom lip caught between her teeth as Matt's impersonal gaze swept from her neck to her feet and back up again, that what he was getting at finally sunk in. Nikolai Dubikov was only attracted to younger women. *Beautiful* younger women, she mentally amended.

At twenty-six, she was definitely a few years short of Dubikov's forty-three—which, she supposed, would at least put her in the right age category. She didn't quite fit that other qualifier, though. Having been labeled "cute" in high school, it had come as something of a relief when she'd finally matured to passably pretty. No one ever took a "cute" person seriously. But beautiful? No way. There were some areas where a woman had to be realistic and that was one of them.

It did, however, come as something of a shock to think Matt might regard her as more than reasonably attractive. As far as Eden had ever been able to tell, he'd never really noticed her at all. Certain she'd have felt flattered had he not looked so accusing, she dismissed both that thought and the corresponding racing of her pulse as inconsequential. What mattered at the moment was that he was beginning to annoy her.

"I know how to handle myself," she defended, crossing her arms to block his view of the fourth button on her mint-green blouse. "And if you're thinking what I think you're thinking, you don't have a thing to worry about. I'm not Mr. Dubikov's type."

"I don't suppose you thought you were that earl's type, either," Matt muttered.

"What earl?"

"The one the president of France probably asked Queen Elizabeth to demote to serf after he ransacked Monet's gardens. Just in case you've forgotten, that little gaff cost us a formal apology from our ambassador."

Eden hadn't forgotten. Before she'd even voiced her question, she'd known what he was talking about. Matt, having escorted her and the Snows to a diplomatic function in Giverny, had witnessed the event preceding her transfer back to the States. But why was he bringing that up? Come to think of it, why had he mentioned that other little incident in Rome? Neither had anything to do with Mr. Dubikov.

Tightening her arms, she sent him a level glance. "He didn't 'ransack' anything." It seemed only fair that she should defend the very nice, but embarrassingly ardent, young nobleman who'd made a minor pest of himself by following her around that day. The young man had been so busy pursuing her during the president's tour that he apparently hadn't heard that picking the famous Impressionist's blooms was an offense punishable by the same fate by which Marie Antoinette had met her demise. "All he did was pick a few flowers and—"

"A few *dozen* flowers," Matt interrupted, "which he then presented to you and you got caught with."

"I couldn't help that!"

"That's just my point!"

"What is?"

"Eden," Matt said, looking very much as if he didn't understand why she was having trouble comprehending what to him was so obvious. "The *point* is that I don't want any problems on this tour. I've got enough to worry about without having to keep an eye on you."

The man was making no sense at all. What was there to worry about? As far as she was concerned, Dubikov's visit here was simply a cultural exchange, not international espionage. Yet he was glaring down at her as if she was about to turn traitor and sabotage the whole operation. "Why would you have to keep an eye on me?"

"Because of what I know about you."

"You don't know anything about me," she returned, wanting very much to erase some of the conviction from his expression. He'd read her dossier, but that didn't mean anything. All the dossier contained was background information. To really know a person, you had to talk with her—and during her brief stint at the embassy, she and Matt had never discussed anything deeper than what the pigeons had done to Ambassador Snow's Mercedes.

"I know enough," he muttered, grabbing his jacket from the chair when one of the double doors swung open.

"Hey, Matt, I hate to interrupt, but we'd better get going. You know what the traffic's like around here at five o'clock." A head of thinning, light-brown hair poked around the door. "Hi, Eden."

It wasn't easy, but Eden swallowed enough of her exasperation to manage a smile. Returning Steve Collier's greeting with a quiet "Hi," she bent down for her luggage.

Matt muttered a terse "Where's Dom?" and, straightening the knot in his tie, started toward the door.

"I'm right here," came the reply just before Domingo Velasquez stepped from behind the closed half of the door. His sharp black eyes darted between Eden and Matt's look of grudging resignation. Choosing Eden's rather subdued smile over Matt's less welcoming expression, he grinned as they merged in the hall. "Who won?"

Purposely denying Eden a chance to clarify the teasing question, Matt frowned at Dom. "I'll meet you guys downstairs. Eden," he continued as he started down the corridor, "you go with them."

"Ready?" Steve asked, picking up the suitcase he'd left by the drinking fountain.

"Ready," Eden repeated, feeling slightly less enthusiastic than she had a while ago. "You want to take the stairs or the elevator?"

Steve didn't answer. Matt did. Halting mid step, he swung around, his eyes darting straight to the two-and-a-half-inch heels of her shoes. "The elevator," he ordered. "We're not starting this out with someone in a cast."

Steve and Dom looked at each other, then back at Eden. They shrugged simultaneously. "The boss has spoken," Steve said philosophically, and motioned for Eden to precede them.

Taking the lead, Eden headed toward the bank of elevators around the corner. The stairs would have been faster, but there really wasn't time to argue with Matt. It was probably just as well. Arguing was right up there with housework on her list of unpleasant things to do.

So was eavesdropping.

She wasn't trying to listen to the hushed conversation taking place several steps behind her, but she couldn't help overhearing some of what was being said, including Steve's remark that he'd never seen Matt as upset as he'd been this morning, and Dom's quieter "You can say that again." It was apparent that the two men she'd just met at last week's security briefing knew Matt fairly well. Their furtive whispering also didn't do much for her lagging sense of anticipation.

Until about fifteen minutes ago, Eden couldn't have imagined anything that would ruin her excitement about this tour. Now, thanks to Matt Killian, she felt as if she'd just been sentenced to the longest month of her life. The way Steve and Dom were sympathetically smiling at her while they waited for the elevator didn't help much, either.

"A whole damn month," Matt muttered, trudging down the stairwell, his garment bag slung over his shoulder.

There were others in the department who apparently failed to understand how dangerous a woman like Eden could be. Either that, or they were more inclined than he was to give her the benefit of the doubt. If it hadn't been for the fact that he never backed out once he said he'd do something, he'd have told his boss he'd changed his mind about this assignment the second he'd seen her name on the briefing sheet this morning. It didn't matter that she was an excellent translator. He didn't even care that she knew her public relations stuff inside out. He'd seen her in action before, so he knew she was as well qualified as anyone else who could have been given the assignment.

That was the problem. He'd seen her in action. And, as far as he was concerned, Eden Michaels was nothing but trouble waiting to happen.

Two

___

Hang on a minute. We've got to find somebody." Matt turned from the anxious airport official, and scanned the sea of passengers surging down the concourse. They'd landed in Boston less than five minutes ago and Eden had promptly disappeared.

Jamming his hands into his pockets, he absently rubbed a coin between his forefinger and thumb. It was an old habit, something he did when he was trying to sort out a problem. The motion wasn't easily detected and maybe that was why he did it—because, unlike pacing or wearing worry on your face, no one could tell that you didn't have everything under control. "Where did she go?"

Steve and Dom craned their necks, checking out the bank of telephones and the exit of the women's rest room. "I don't know," Dom mumbled over his shoulder. "All she said was that she'd meet us at the inter-terminal shuttle bus in a few minutes. I know she thought we had plenty of time."

"Had," Matt repeated, wrestling with the logistics of sending Dom down to the rapid-transit station to get her while he and Steve went with the man who'd just told him Dubikov's plane would be landing early. "We did have time, but we don't now. Don't either of you know any Russian?"

"You know we don't." Steve kept up his survey of the crowd, focusing most of his attention on the women coming out of the ladies' room. "Not enough to do us any good, anyway. Maybe we can get someone from the airline to help us out."

"Customs will have somebody," Dom offered patiently.

"Damn it." Refusing to let the complications mount, Matt stuck with the immediate problem. The language barrier wasn't really his major concern at the moment. According to the briefing sheets, Sergei Androvich, the Soviet Ministry of Culture's liaison who'd be acting as Dubikov's manager, spoke English. "Why didn't you stay with her?"

It was apparent from the looks he received from both his men that they hadn't thought Eden needed a baby-sitter. It was equally obvious that they weren't quite ready to reconsider that position.

"Hey!" Jabbing Matt's arm, Dom pointed between a woman pushing a stroller and two businessmen weaving their way through the throng. "There she is."

At Matt's terse "Let's go," all three men surged forward, the airport representative fast on their heels.

Eden left the small gift shop, juggling bag, briefcase and purse to check her watch. Since the department had arranged to have the bulk of their luggage picked up for them they had avoided the hassle of the claim area. All they had to do now was catch the shuttle bus to the international terminal and kill the next forty-five minutes waiting for Du-bikov.

She'd expected to be a little nervous. After all, it wasn't every day that a person met a celebrity. But the small knot of anxiety in her stomach didn't seem to have anything to do with meeting the great violinist. It did, however, have everything to do with the man who'd just grabbed her arm and was practically running with her.

"The next time you decide to take off," Matt muttered tightly, "tell somebody where you're going. Dom, take her bag."

There was no time for Eden to tell Matt she was quite capable of carrying her travel bag herself. Without missing a step as they darted past groups of gaping passengers, Dom lifted the strap from her shoulder and slung it over his. Steve and another man in a light-gray suit shot ahead of them.

Bent on keeping up with Matt, who, for all practical purposes, looked like he'd drag her if she dared to slow down, she directed her remarkably calm inquiry to the muscle bunched in his jaw. "What's going on?"

"Dubikov's flight's early."

Something in his tone made it sound as if she were personally responsible for the plane being ahead of schedule. Graciously attributing his testiness to the fact that he was in a hurry, she occupied herself with the task of ignoring his insistent grip on her arm. She was also trying to figure out where they were going. They'd just taken a wrong turn. "The shuttle's the other way."

"We're not taking it. They've got a car for us outside."

Within the minute, they passed through a short, bare hall and out a door marked Do Not Enter. Inhaling the damp evening air, Eden saw Dom grab Matt's bag and toss it into the open trunk of a white sedan. Seconds later, she was being pushed into the back seat, Dom getting in on one side and Matt sliding in alongside her. Steve and the man in the gray suit practically dove into the front seat, and all four doors closed at once.

Just as Eden was thinking that this was the kind of crazy scene that occurred only in movies, the car lurched forward and sped away. Under any other circumstances, she'd probably have found the whole thing rather exhilarating. The State Department, though, wouldn't find it at all amusing if Dubikov didn't receive a proper welcome. In a way she was grateful for the rush. Now she wouldn't have time to get nervous over meeting Mr. Dubikov.

That thought was fine, but it didn't begin to explain why the size of the knot in her stomach had doubled.

The back seat would have held two people quite comfortably—even two men the size of those on either side of her. But add a third person and it got rather...cozy.

It wasn't Dom's thigh against hers that bothered her; it was the solid leg pressed against her on the other side. And the fact that, unlike Dom, Matt hadn't made any effort to give her more room.

Intent on pretending she didn't notice the feel of those steely muscles, or the way he'd just thrown his arm over the back of the seat, she pulled a small, flat sack from the side pocket of her purse and forced herself not to think about the hard object she'd just felt. With Matt's left arm behind her, she was tucked against his side, his gun poking her arm. She knew all three of the men were wearing shoulder holsters. She'd seen them when they'd presented their identification in the airline's operations center just before boarding the plane by way of the pilot's air stairs.

Though she accepted the side arms as part and parcel of an agent's job, she still couldn't help edging away a little. "Give these to your nephew," she said to Dom who, after staring at the package in Eden's hand for a moment, appeared to know exactly what was inside it.

"Is that what you were doing? Buying these?" he asked with a grin. "Thanks."

Eden nodded, far more aware than she wanted to be of the way her shoulder fit into the groove of Matt's arm. It was dumb, really dumb even to be thinking about that. Had it been Dom's arm, or Steve's, she wouldn't have given it any thought at all.

"Postcards." Dom leaned forward a little, slipping the sack into the inside pocket of his suit jacket as he looked over at Matt. "My nephew collects them. He's always asking me to bring him some, and I'm always forgetting."

"How'd she know about that?" Matt asked, directing the question right past Eden as the car banked around a corner.

"Not all of us slept on the plane," Steve drawled from the front. "Some of us found more interesting things to do."

"Like pick on the flight attendant," Eden supplied, adding Matt's scowl to the list of things she was ignoring.

Steve chuckled. "She was great, wasn't she?"

Dom frowned at the back of Steve's head. "I think they're trained to be nice to obnoxious, bald men."

"I'm not bald. My hairline's just receding a little."

"Yeah. To the back of your neck."

Like Dom, Steve was somewhere around thirty, but, to Eden, his thinning hair made him look a little older. More in line with what she figured Matt to be—closer to thirty-five. Without thinking about it, she glanced at him, subconsciously wanting to confirm that guess.

Her innate curiosity was immediately overridden by the quick change in his expression. He'd actually been smiling at the gibes his men were trading and, for a moment, it looked as though he was about to add his two cents' worth. But the instant he caught her eye, his smile flattened.

"Are those our limos?" he asked the driver, as they pulled up beside two long black vehicles.

It didn't take any great powers of perception for Eden to know that Matt wasn't too pleased with her. It was also quite obvious that he didn't mind letting her know it. It would have been awfully nice, though, to find out what she'd done to cause his annoyance. While Steve and Dom waited for the driver to unlock an unmarked terminal door, Matt stood back watching her. Not about to let him know that she found his cool glare more than a little intimidating, she forced a bravado she really didn't feel.

"Is something wrong?" she inquired politely.

With a cryptic "Not yet," he stepped forward, taking her arm when the door swung open. "Come on."

She didn't quite know what to make of that terribly unenlightening response, or the tiny frisson of heat generated by the simple touch of his hand on her elbow. Since Matt didn't seem to notice anything peculiar about the casual gesture, she decided not to pay any attention to it, either. There were other things to think about. "What about the press?"

Matt glanced at his watch, propelling her forward at a more reasonable pace than the one he'd set a few minutes before. "If they don't show up in the next few minutes, they can forget about talking to Dubikov tonight. We're not hanging around here to wait for them."

Eden knew that airports weren't security agents' favorite places. There were too many potential safety risks. That was why, from this point on, all air transportation would be in a State Department jet with military pilots.

She also knew that Harry wanted to keep questions from the media to a minimum this evening. Thinking she'd never be able to do better than to have those questions avoided entirely, she nodded agreeably at Matt. "In that case, I'll just get the introductions out of the way, then tell them we're going to the hotel. Do you want us in one car and them in another?"

The lines in his forehead eased, a fair indication that he wasn't going to let personal aggravations interfere with the business at hand. Concerned only with coordinating their departure, he became quite civil. After telling her he thought it best to keep at least one of his men with Dubikov, he said, "You ride in the lead car with him, one of his bodyguards and Dom. I'll be in the car behind you with everyone else."

He released his grip on her arm and motioned her ahead of him when they reached a spacious and comfortably furnished VIP lounge. Intent on ignoring the sensation of lingering heat beneath the smooth fabric of her suit sleeve, she didn't quite catch the subtle tension that slipped back into his voice.

"Remember what I told you, Eden."

"About what?" she asked, but Matt didn't get a chance to clarify his quiet admonition. The delegation from Russia was funnelling through the door.

Eden recognized the neatly bearded Nikolai Dubikov instantly. He wasn't as tall as the two dark-suited and somber bodyguards behind him, but he wasn't a small man by any means. Stocky and barrel-chested, he was a rather imposing presence in a suddenly quiet room. The consummate artist, he wore a demeanor of superiority that required deference—something the thin, bespectacled and very solemn gentleman who appeared at his side carrying a violin case could never hope to achieve. In a way, Mr. Dubikov seemed every bit as arrogant as Matt, but on a much more aristocratic and refined level. He didn't have Matt's bearing of subdued aggression or his air of silent command. And he certainly didn't have his rugged, blatantly masculine appeal.

The moment she'd been looking forward to for weeks had finally arrived. Now that it was here, Eden felt a little cheated. Instead of thinking about how excited she was to finally meet Mr. Dubikov, her thoughts were being interfered with by the man whose darkly attractive features were set in a mask of reserve.

Refusing to let him ruin this momentous occasion for her, she stepped forward, her mind occupied with the task of translating her thoughts into Russian. Since the terms Mr., Mrs. and Miss had no counterpart in that language, she addressed Nikolai Dubikov by his first and last names, as was the proper form of formal address. She smiled as she spoke first to the man whose talent she so admired, then to the gentleman beside him. To her infinite relief, Mr. Dubikov's brown eyes lit up with an impishness that was completely unexpected, and his mustache lifted with an engaging grin. Sergei Androvich, his manager, merely nodded.

It didn't take long for official greetings to be exchanged or to translate introductions between the men. Within ten minutes, all that needed to be said had been, and everyone was heading through the lounge toward the door. Eden hung back, frowning as she watched Steve and Dom lead the new arrivals outside.

Matt was halfway across the room when he stopped short. "Something the matter?"

"Oh, ah...not really," she returned, picking up her purse from one of the long sofas. Though Matt didn't exactly look impatient, she knew he was in a hurry to get out of here.

"That's not the impression I get." Stepping in front of her to block her exit, Matt crossed his arms over the impressive breadth of his chest. "Ever since Androvich spoke to you,

you've seemed a little preoccupied. What were you two talking about?''

Mr. Dubikov's manager, who had proved to be nowhere near as docile as he'd first appeared, had taken her aside while the other men made sure their luggage was accounted for. The conversation that Mr. Androvich commenced in heavily accented English had been quick and to the point. "He just wanted to make sure the arrangements were still the same."

"That's all?"

She nodded, thinking that any second now Matt would let her rejoin the others. Instead, he merely tilted his head. Clearly, he wasn't going to budge until she'd given him a more acceptable reason for her preoccupation.

She almost forgot that reason. For once he wasn't frowning at her, but what he was doing was almost as disconcerting. There was interest in his incredibly blue eyes, a kind of grudging curiosity that only increased as his gaze slowly worked its way over her face. When Matt's eyes narrowed a little as they reached her mouth, she finally said, "His English is excellent," certain he was interested in hearing only what she had to say about Androvich. "I got the feeling he wanted me to know that. He also wanted to make sure I understood he'd be sitting with Mr. Dubikov at all the press conferences."

Matt shrugged. "Androvich is just doing his job," he returned casually, his glance straying to the delicate hollow of her throat. "And part of his job is to make sure your translations are accurate. Especially about anything political. They may have agreed to allow an American to deal with our press and public but he's from their ministry. You know that."

Some people would have taken offense at Matt's frank explanation. Not Eden. She was far too confident of her skills to be insulted at the thought of having her interpretations monitored. What bothered her now was what necessitated that kind of thing. "I guess I'd forgotten about the significance of Mr. Androvich's Party affiliation," she admitted apolitically. "It's really kind of sad, isn't it?"

"What is?"

"That lack of trust."

Eden had never considered herself to be terribly complex. But her simple statement changed the vaguely distracted light in Matt's eyes to one of total absorption. He was studying her openly now, his unveiled scrutiny making her feel like some odd specimen that thoroughly confused him. "That's just the way things are."

"But it doesn't have to be that way," she gently refuted.

His glance slowly moved from her mouth back to her eyes. Try as she might, she could see nothing but skepticism in those mysteriously veiled depths. "You can't possibly be that naive."

"I don't think believing in people is naive."

"Fine," he returned agreeably enough, and if she hadn't known better she'd have sworn she saw the light of a teasing smile flash across his face. "We'll just call it foolish."

"Why do I have the feeling you aren't listening to me?"

"Probably because I've had a few more years' experience along these lines than you have. Suspicion is something you learn to accept," he told her, a note of remorse beneath his hard-edged cynicism.

"You may accept it, but I won't."

"You will," he assured her. "It comes with the territory."

He turned away but not quickly enough. Eden knew he hadn't meant for her to see the hint of regret shadowing his face—or maybe Matt hadn't even been aware of it himself. Between that and the look of mild amusement she had glimpsed a moment ago, she almost forgot what he'd said about how her basic trust in people would change.

Telling herself she didn't have time to think about that now, she entered the cordoned-off area outside the private lounge. The porters had arrived with a cart full of luggage, and Mr. Dubikov was at the door of the second limousine, obviously unable to understand what Matt was trying to tell him. Knowing Matt wanted him to ride in the first car with her, she intervened. "Nikolai Dubikov," she began, only to have the violinist cut her off with a shake of his head.

Her fear that somehow she'd done something wrong was instantly compounded by Matt's sharp glance. More concerned with the frown on Mr. Dubikov's face than the one on Matt's, she swallowed uneasily and looked up as the famous musician took her hand.

It was with no small amount of relief that she discovered the problem.

Speaking in Russian since he knew very little English, he gave her a little bow. "I must ask you a favor. All the beautiful women I know address me as 'Niki.' I would be most honored if you will call me by that name. And, please, what is this gentleman trying to say?"

She smiled into his gentle brown eyes, thinking his reputation with women was well-earned. He was suave, urbane and looked so incredibly sincere that no female on earth would even think to question what was probably his oldest and most used line. Matt, she thought, should be taking notes.

After acknowledging the very flattering request, Eden quickly explained what "the gentleman" wanted. After gravely bowing over her hand, the violinist proceeded to his assigned car.

"Would you mind telling me what that was all about?" Matt demanded.

"He wants me to call him Niki," she said with a shrug, and hurried after the man in question. "See you at the hotel." Wanting nothing more than to escape the blue eyes following her every move, she slid into the front seat of the limo. She couldn't close the door, though. Dom was holding it.

"The mobile phone in the second car isn't working," she heard him advise Matt. "It was fine when you had Steve and me check it out a while ago, but now all we get is static or dead air. The driver said another car could be here in about twenty minutes if you think it's necessary to wait."

Matt apparently didn't want to wait. Dom slid in beside her and a moment later, the two long, black vehicles pulled out into the starless Boston night.

It wasn't until they'd been driving at least five minutes that Matt allowed himself to relax. Not completely; just enough to let his shoulders drop and relieve some of the tension in his neck. Even with the unexpected early arrival of Dubikov's plane, everything was under control. Everything except Eden, he thought, catching a glimpse of her head in the car ahead of him. Though she'd handled herself with a professionalism he couldn't criticize, something about her seemed to defy convention. Something about her seemed to defy *him*.

Matt knew he'd been pretty irritable with her earlier. He always got edgy when he was tired. That's why he'd excused himself for snapping her head off when she'd come out of the gift shop. He wished he could as easily dismiss the way she made him feel—a little off balance. The last time he'd felt that unprepared, he'd been ducking Molotov cocktails while trying to get a diplomat out of a small, now-nonexistent country. Being around Eden was a little like that explosive situation. One never quite knew when—

"What in the..?"

His words, like his thoughts, were cut off as he bolted forward in his seat. The hotel was only three blocks ahead, but the car Eden and Dubikov were in had just made a squealing left turn on to the next street. "Follow them," he ordered, his voice tight with the same control he always exerted over himself.

"There is problem?" Androvich, who was sandwiched between Steve and one of Dubikov's linebacker-size bodyguards, inquired as their car swerved around the corner.

There wasn't any problem. Not as far as Eden was concerned. "It's just a few more blocks," she offered blandly, pointing to the upcoming intersection. "Take a left at the light."

The uniformed chauffeur nodded, accelerating as he changed lanes.

"Hey! Wait a minute!" Dom dropped the map he was holding, and looked backward to see if the car behind them had made the corner. "We've got to clear this with Matt first."

"How could we? Niki didn't ask to see where tomorrow night's concert would be held until just now."

"We can pull over and tell him," Dom pointed out, then instructed the driver to stop as soon as he could.

Eden turned around, her glance darting between Niki and the hulk sharing the back seat. No one in Matt's car was frantically motioning them over, so it seemed safe to assume that everything was all right. "I don't think it's necessary. Besides, with all this traffic, we couldn't pull over without getting into an accident." Satisfied with that bit of logic, she reached down to pick up the map. She was halfway up when her quiet "Uh-oh" was muffled by the gasps coming from either side of her.

The whole thing was over in a matter of seconds. Intent on making the light, the driver stepped on the gas as he entered the turn lane. Matt's car swung from behind them, presumably to pull ahead. A little blue Volkswagen waiting for the signal to change jumped the light, the police car behind him right on his bumper. All four cars came to a crunching halt smack-dab in the middle of one of Boston's busiest intersections.

Eden didn't know who hit whom first. All she knew for sure was that her head bumped the dashboard. The dashboard was padded. The little brass plate announcing the make of this particular vehicle was not. There were also some rather interesting white spots dancing over the floor mat.

The stars vanished as quickly as they'd appeared. There were, it seemed, some advantages to having a hard head. In the literal sense, anyway.

"Is everyone all right?" she asked, momentarily forgetting that half of the men staring at the pink cloud billowing up from the radiator couldn't understand her. Rubbing her head, she squinted at the strangely colored phenomenon. A moment later, she realized it was the flashing red light from the police car that gave the steam that pastel tint.

It didn't take long to learn that no one had been hurt. But because their horn was stuck it did take some effort for Eden to hear the conversation taking place between Matt, the irate owner of the Volkswagen, and the cop who looked like he was ready to call in reinforcements when one of Niki's bodyguards started insisting, in Russian, that Mr. Dubikov be taken to the hotel immediately.

Pulling her jacket tightly around her to ward off the chill of the late January evening, and shivering as much from nerves as the dampness in the air, Eden skirted the fender against which Niki, his other guard, and his tight-lipped manager were leaning. Niki appeared quite content to stand there on the outskirts, viewing the chaos. Androvich, though, looked like he'd much rather be in the middle of the mess than stuck there keeping Niki company. Only Eden seemed to share Niki's decision to remain uninvolved.

"Eden! Get over here!"

At Matt's sharp command, Eden raised her eyes in a silent prayer for mercy. It was too soon for him to have figured out what had happened so she really didn't need to worry yet. But it was always a good idea to enter the fray with the best reinforcement available.

"Eden!"

"Coming," she called back, then stopped when Niki touched her arm. Matt no doubt wanted her to translate the increasingly insistent demands coming from his Russian counterpart, but that would have to wait for a minute. Niki was holding out a neatly folded white handkerchief.

"You are bleeding," Androvich offered, when Niki said nothing.

"Eden!"

With a grateful smile, Eden pressed the handkerchief to the small cut above her left eyebrow, withdrawing it to see a little blood. Then, telling both men she'd be right back, she hastened to answer that third, and much louder, command.

The commotion greeting her reminded Eden of children who hadn't yet learned that it is not polite to interrupt. Since Matt was occupied with the task of trying to get a word in edgewise between the policeman and the angry driver of the Volkswagen, Eden turned to the tall and tensely solemn Russian who looked for all the world as if he was ready to claim his luggage and catch the next plane back to the motherland.

Tersely, he explained what he wanted to Eden and she passed the request on to Matt.

"Is there any way we can get Niki to the hotel? It isn't necessary for him and the rest of his party to wait while this gets cleared up, and this gentleman is concerned with the present lack of security. Not," she hastened to add, "that he thinks anything will happen. But he says he has rules to follow...and they're all pretty tired."

Matt hadn't even glanced at her. His eyes, dangerously cold, had fixed on the driver of the first limousine. "No one's going anywhere until I find out why you didn't stick to the route. I want to know where you were going, and who gave the order."

Dom stood beside the cringing driver, looking absolutely miserable. "It wasn't a kidnap attempt," he said resignedly.

Like any department employee who'd been assigned to an embassy in the last few years, Eden had taken the mandatory course on kidnappings and terrorism, but it wasn't until that moment that she fully comprehended why Matt looked so frightening. In her opinion the current situation hadn't warranted much thought on that particular matter. She could only wonder at the workings of a security agent's mind. Did they always jump to the worst possible conclusions like this?

Graciously allowing that it was the nature of the men's job to expect what she hadn't even thought about, she started to cut in right after Matt's growled, "Then explain what it was."

Dom helped her out. "It's all okay," he said, his glance darting to Eden as if to say he'd take care of this. "Dubikov wanted to see Symphony Hall and since it was just a few blocks away, Eden told—"

"Eden!" Matt exploded, bringing everyone to a sudden silence. "She's responsible for this?"

"Come on, Matt," Dom coaxed calmly, but reasoning with a man who looked as if his blood pressure had just surpassed the height of the thirty-story bank building on the corner was a total impossibility.

"I should have known. Damn it," Matt snapped, turning the full force of those accusing blue eyes on the woman whose unconscious attempt at retreat was halted by the large frame looming behind her. "They haven't even been here for half an hour and already you've—"

"She didn't really—"

Cutting off Dom's attempt to defend her, Matt glared down at the top of her head. The man behind her hadn't moved. "She can speak for herself, Domingo."

Eden blinked up at him, refusing to back down or to give him the satisfaction of an argument. There was no point in arguing with him, anyway. He wouldn't hear a word she'd say. Without even giving her a chance, he'd already formed some very close-minded and, to her way of thinking, unfair opinion of her, and he was just pigheaded enough to hang on to that conviction no matter what she said or did.

"Well?" he prodded when she'd done nothing but stand there staring up at him.

"Well, what?"

"Aren't you going to defend yourself?"

Thinking his perfectly straight white teeth would certainly shatter if he clenched his jaw any harder, she calmly balled Niki's handkerchief in her fist. "Why should I? You've already decided you're going to be mad at me."

Intent on ignoring Matt's order to come back, she squeezed between Dom and Niki's bodyguard. Matt was right on her heels.

She got no farther than the front of the damaged limo before a large hand clamped over her shoulder. That hand was immediately withdrawn when, half a step later, she stopped near the crowd gathering on the sidewalk. Matt swung around in front of her, apparently not caring that the size of their audience had just increased.

"Dom said no one got hurt."

"No one did," she returned, wondering what he was trying to pin on her now. No matter what approach he took, she wasn't going to discuss this with him any further. He clearly failed to see that this whole mess was as much his fault as hers. If he'd just followed instead of trying to cut them off at the intersection . . .

"You did."

The quieter note that had slipped into his voice seemed to relieve a bit of his irritation. Not by much, though, Eden thought. The way he shoved his hands into his pockets indicated that was probably the only way he could keep them from closing around her neck.

"It's just a little cut," she assured him, unconsciously touching her throat. "Our car got the worst of it. I don't think it's drivable."

He continued to study the tiny wound above her eyebrow. She wasn't sure, but something that almost looked like concern flickered through his expression. The hard line of his mouth softened, his dark brows drawing together. Several seconds passed before he spoke, but when he did, she was sure any concern she might have imagined was only for the disabled vehicle.

"Not with a hole in the radiator. It'll have to be towed."

"A truck's on its way," Steve said from behind Matt. "The cop just called for one. Think we can all fit in one car?"

Both men glanced at the vehicle they'd been riding in. Somehow it had escaped with nothing more than minor dents in the right front and left rear fenders. "Yeah, I think so,... if you stay here with me to straighten this all out. The men will fit, but Eden will have to sit on somebody's lap."

Eden didn't want to sit on anyone's lap. "Maybe I should walk. It's not that far."

"You'll ride," Matt informed her, reverting to that formidable scowl he executed so well. "Go tell Dubikov's people what we're doing."

Yes, your lordship, she answered silently, thinking him as authoritarian as any dictator she'd ever met while she wandered off to do his bidding. The man had all the finesse and sensitivity of Genghis Khan.

As autocratic as he'd been, Eden was silently thankful for Matt's insistence that she go with the others. By the time she and Dom had accompanied the four extremely tired travelers to the elegant old hotel where they'd be staying for the next three nights, and escorted them to their lavishly appointed rooms, the nagging little pain in her head was threatening to escalate into a full-blown ache. Preferring to think it was caused by Matt rather than her encounter with the dashboard, Eden downed two headache tablets after dutifully telling Harry's answering machine that they'd arrived. Then she sank down on the huge, king-size bed.

For several seconds she sat frowning at the Currier and Ives prints that went nicely with the turn of the century replicas furnishing her room. Ordinarily, she'd have appreciated the detail in the remarkably authentic reproductions. But this wasn't ordinarily. It wasn't what had happened a while ago that made the situation seem less than normal. As far as Eden was concerned almost everything was just fine. Niki had gallantly brushed off her profuse apologies for the inconvenience and promptly invited her to join him and his entourage for a glass of champagne to celebrate their arrival. Eden had known she couldn't refuse because the Russians put great stock in the social custom of the shared drink. Even Niki's companions, who'd opted for vodka instead of the sparkling wine, had accepted the unfortunate incident as one of those things that happen, then changed the subject. Matt, though, had been a whole other story.

She should have finished that glass of champagne. It might have helped her headache, she told herself, then promptly dismissed the thought. "Should haves" were something she didn't spend much time on. After all, what was past was past and that applied to everything from an abandoned glass of champagne to the class in archaeology she'd once wanted to take. Eden much preferred to deal with the present, and presently she was trying to figure out how one got along with a person whose narrow-mindedness was surpassed only by his arrogance.

"I liked him better in Italy," she muttered, rubbing her head. There, Matt had treated her with polite indifference, shown her the same reserve he'd displayed toward the rest of the sizable staff. Now he was being neither polite nor indifferent, and was proving himself to be slightly impossible in the process.

Still thinking Matt much nicer when she hadn't had to work with him, she reached over to answer the insistent summons of the telephone. She hoped it wasn't Harry.

"Eden? It's Matt. I want to see you."

Three

I want to see you," Eden repeated, mimicking Matt's baritone after she'd hung up the phone. He hadn't said, May I see you? Or even asked if his timing was convenient. He wanted to see her and, therefore, he would.

It hadn't occurred to Eden to refuse his terse summons, not until after he'd broken the connection, anyway. The command in his voice hadn't allowed room for disobedience, and he had hung up before she could consider whether or not *she* wanted to see *him*.

Feeling quite spineless at having met his order with nothing more assertive than a quiet "Okay," she shrugged. The inevitable, she supposed, couldn't be postponed forever. Until the air was cleared between Matt and her, she wouldn't be able to enjoy anything about this tour. She always maintained good relationships with her co-workers and, so far, she seemed to be getting along just fine with everyone else. She'd get along with Matt if it killed her.

Half convinced that she'd just sentenced herself to a very short life, she stepped out into the deserted hall as if she were on her way to the gallows.

Straightening her shoulders, Eden picked up her pace. The women in the Michaels family weren't cowards, she reminded herself. Grandma Michaels had gone head to head with the incredibly stubborn mayor of Dew Glen, Iowa, over water rights, then turned the town council on its ear by securing that office for herself after the mayor refused to take her seriously. Aunt Jenna Michaels, her dad's youngest sister and a marine biologist, spent most of her time swimming around in tanks filled with sharks.

Eden had no political aspirations whatsoever—and just viewing a great white from the other side of a tank gave her the creeps. But with that kind of heritage, she should certainly be able to hold her own against a brick wall named Matthew Killian.

At least that brick wall had a sense of propriety. Instead of showing up at her door and putting her in the awkward position of being alone with him in her hotel room, Matt, as he said he would be, was waiting for her in the lounge area just off the elevator. He was sitting slumped in one of the two white leather wing chairs facing each other over a low, claw-footed table. As she approached, Eden saw him glance toward her, then push his fingers through his windblown hair as he wearily rose. The man looked exhausted.

Eden had assumed he'd called her from his room, the one she understood he'd be sharing with Dom. Seeing his overcoat on the table beside the red house phone on the table and his travel bag occupying the other chair, it was apparent he hadn't gotten that far. Realizing that he hadn't even taken the time to settle in before summoning her didn't do a whole lot for her courage. Obviously, his reason for this meeting had taken priority.

Certain that reason dealt with the mess back at the intersection, she wasn't at all prepared for his quiet "Are you sure you're all right?"

Eden tried to mask her momentary incomprehension. But what she saw only served to increase it. He didn't seem angry at all, and the concern she thought she'd only imagined before was quite apparent. He actually seemed to be worried about her, and that did something very strange to her heart. The most notable effect was the slight acceleration of its beat.

Caught completely off guard, she could only watch when Matt raised his hand to lift the feathery hair brushing her eyebrows. His fingers barely grazed her skin, but that slight contact was enough to demand some kind of response.

The sharp breath she drew brought with it the subtle essence of after-shave. Somehow, that faintly spicy scent managed to compound the effect of his unexpected touch. "I told you I was fine," she heard herself say, as his free hand skimmed past her shoulder.

There were calluses ridging the base of his fingers. She felt them just before his palm cupped the back of her neck to bring her closer.

"Turn around here to the light. There. That's better."

"Matt," she began, convinced he had no idea how his voice had gentled. He seemed perfectly oblivious to anything but his very unnecessary examination of what was nothing more than a tiny scratch. "I said I'm—"

"I know what you said, but I want to see for myself."

Stubborn. The man could definitely be stubborn. "All right," she conceded, allowing him a couple of seconds to scrutinize her nearly infinitesimal injury. "You've seen it now, and I really do appreciate your concern, but what else did you want?"

She really wasn't in any great hurry to resume the discussion she'd refused to finish a while ago, but she wasn't about to let him disarm her any further. Checking on her welfare was probably only a ploy to weaken her defenses before moving in for the kill, she thought, remembering once again her Aunt Jenna's silent but deadly pets.

It seemed to Eden that Matt appeared to be giving her question more consideration than was necessary as his narrowed eyes quietly skimmed her face. His gaze drifted slowly from her forehead, coming to rest on the fullness of her lips. For a moment, he appeared quite fascinated with their slightly breathless part, his preoccupation revealing itself when the pressure of his hand increased almost imperceptibly against the back of her neck. It felt as if his fingers had moved upward, insinuating themselves into the silky hair at her nape.

Eden didn't move. She saw him draw a long, slow and very controlled breath when he raised his eyes to meet hers. For a full three seconds he simply stared down at her while her pulse accelerated and the floor beneath her feet underwent a subtle shift.

"What else do I want?" he repeated as if weighing any number of intriguing options. Then, without warning, the corners of his mouth tightened, and the vaguely disconcerted look gave way to his usual decisiveness when he jerked them back to the small cut above the soft arch of her eyebrow. "Nothing at the moment," he said flatly.

The combination of relief and disappointment flickering through Eden's expression spoke fairly well of the chaos his heavy-lidded perusal had caused. Doing her best to make sure he didn't see how heavily she was leaning toward the latter, she concentrated on magnifying her relief. Apparently, he wasn't going to start yelling at her again. "You could have just asked me how I was on the phone."

Her attempt to sound accusing didn't work. All she succeeded in doing was letting him hear the faint tremor in her voice. She found it extremely disturbing that it was even there.

She remained perfectly still, as if to prove to herself that Matt was not affecting her the way she thought he was. Attempts at self-delusion rarely worked for her, but she held her ground. She really had no choice. Her knees felt about as stable as one of her infamous soufflés. One step and she'd probably collapse.

Looking very much as if he'd just realized that his purpose had already been accomplished, Matt finally withdrew his hands. When he had them pushed into the safety of his pockets, he gave her an absent shrug. "I told you, I wanted to see for myself. I was afraid you'd need a stitch or something, but it doesn't look that bad. Ice should take care of the swelling."

"You wouldn't happen to have been born in Missouri, would you?"

He didn't even blink. "No."

Most people would have gone on to ask the reason for such an off-the-wall question, or automatically supplied the correct information. Not Matt. He simply stood there frowning at her.

"I just thought you might have been," she went on, determined to make her point with or without his cooperation.

"Why would you think that?"

"Because you obviously can't take a person's word."

"You're a little quick to form judgments, aren't you?"

Crossing her arms in a gesture that could be interpreted as either defensive or protective, and not caring which way he saw it, she tipped her head back. "Actually, I don't think

I am. If anything, I'm inclined to give a person the benefit of the doubt."

Twice, Matt thought, balling his hands in his pockets. Twice now, she'd nailed him with an insight that made him a little uncomfortable. First, she'd quite correctly informed him that he'd decided to be mad at her before she'd ever had a chance to do anything wrong. And, now, she'd caught him with his own accusation. He found her perception a little unsettling.

He'd always thought himself to be fair, but when it came to Eden he seemed to lose all objectivity. A minute ago, when he'd felt her pulse race beneath his fingers and seen her refusal to acknowledge the sensual pull flowing between them, he'd almost lost a good deal of his common sense, too.

"That's a nice sentiment, but I prefer to form my opinion after a person's proved himself."

"If what you said back at the airport is any indication, it could take forever for a person to prove himself to your satisfaction."

"Sometimes it does."

Eden eyed him dully. There was no sense beating around the bush when diving through the middle was the shorter route. Choosing that path, though, usually meant encountering a few scratchy limbs. In Matt's case, it was more like the trunk of an unyielding oak. "Would you mind telling me how one goes about meeting your criteria, then? At least that way, I'll have a fighting chance. Which," she added hastily, "is something you've refused to give me. I feel like I've been tried and convicted, but nobody's bothered to tell me what I've been charged with."

"How about failure to follow the rules?" he suggested.

"Bending rules isn't the same as breaking them," she defended, certain she knew what he was referring to. "Dom had just started to explain what happened when you—"

"There's more to it than that," he cut in sharply.

"More to what?"

"More to why I already knew you'd cause trouble even before you proved it." Glancing over his shoulder to make sure they were still alone, he lowered his voice to a shouting whisper. "Hasn't it ever occurred to you that things happen when you're around? I honestly don't think you cause problems on purpose, but you've got to admit that 'uneventful' does not describe your year and a half with the department."

She did have to admit that. She wasn't, however, going to give Matt any satisfaction by doing so verbally. "You said you'd read my dossier," she whispered back. "If you'd read far enough, you'd know I've been exonerated in all those incidents. They could have happened to anybody."

"But things like that *don't* happen to everybody. They happen to you. Just like that fiasco an hour ago. You were supposed to stick to the route."

"If I'd known you'd pull the cloak-and-dagger stuff by trying to cut our car off, I would have! I was told to be as accommodating as possible and I hardly thought driving past the place Niki wanted to see was anything terribly extraordinary. It wasn't like he wanted a tour of the docks or something."

"Why didn't you clear it with me first?"

"Because if we'd tried to pull over in all that traffic, it might have caused an accident!"

"What in the hell do you think that was at Boylston and Copley Square? The Boston Tea Party?"

The breath Eden inhaled was definitely shaky. Not trembling like those she'd drawn while Matt had been touching her. She was far too agitated even to think about that now. But it was unsteady enough for her to realize that she was more than just a little irritated with the man glaring down at her.

The fact that she had been arguing with him quite blatantly didn't even occur to her until five whole seconds went by without a word passing between them. Something happened in those seconds, but as Eden watched the little lines at the corners of Matt's eyes deepen, and caught a glimpse of what she could have sworn was a smile when Matt turned away, she had absolutely no idea what it was.

Matt knew. He'd just realized that if he didn't walk away from her right now, he'd probably wind up doing something incredibly stupid. The thought of her reaction to what he was contemplating was what made it so difficult to suppress his grin.

His fatigue had finally caught up with him. That had to be why he'd stood there thinking about taking her in his arms to shut her up. Something about her seemed to demand that kind of response from him and, since he didn't have the energy to fight both her and himself at the moment, a strategic retreat was the only viable option.

"I'd like to continue this discussion," he informed her, his tone surprisingly normal, "but frankly, I'm too tired." Picking up his bag and slinging it over his shoulder, he started down the hall. "Oh, Eden," he called back, "from now on you'll ride with me. I think it will be safer that way."

Damn him. Damn him! she thought all the way back to her room. She'd let him goad her into an argument, then he had sauntered off halfway through it as if nothing were more important than his sleep. He'd even had the audacity to laugh at her—although, she supposed, she should give him some credit for trying to hide that.

Not feeling quite that generous, she plopped down on the edge of her bed. She'd left this room determined to get along with him and come back to find that purpose thoroughly defeated.

Well, maybe not thoroughly, Eden told herself, reaching down to pull off her shoes. There was always tomorrow, and by tomorrow, she was sure she'd forget all about that one incredibly thrilling, definitely unnerving moment when she'd thought he was about to kiss her.

The human mind was truly unreliable. It seemed the harder a person tried to forget something, the more firmly the unwanted thought took root. Eden hadn't been awake for more than ten seconds the next morning when the memory of how Matt's eyes had darkened when he'd focused on her mouth sent her scurrying from her bed. It usually took a long shower and at least one cup of coffee for coherence to kick in. Now, after calling room service for the coffee and heading into the bathroom, she was forced to admit she was already wide awake.

"Why am I thinking about him?" she muttered, frowning into the mirror as she peered at her left eyebrow. The cut was really no big deal. The skin beneath it wasn't even swollen, and her bangs would cover the tiny scratch. "I've got other things to think about."

Those other things started with a press conference due to begin at nine-thirty in the hotel's Patriot Room. Niki was then to have lunch in his suite with the conductor of the Boston Symphony. Right after that was a rehearsal with the orchestra, which could take anywhere from four to six hours. Since Niki was notoriously demanding when it came to his accompaniment, Eden wouldn't be at all surprised if that six hours extended to seven. No matter how long it took, she had to be there, always available to translate.

If Matt's presence weren't also necessary, she might have looked forward to the day with a bit more anticipation. As it was, she felt only a twinge of her former excitement and, forty-five minutes later, a great deal of determination. Giving her freshly dried hair one last flick with the brush, then downing the last of her coffee, she pushed her toes into her pumps. It might take some doing, but she *would* get along with him—whether he liked it or not.

It wasn't long before she had to practice what she'd preached. Seeing Matt outside the gold and green Patriot Room, she smiled. "Did you sleep well?"

For a moment, he simply glanced down the row of fabric-covered buttons running the length of her teal-blue suede dress. His survey continued past the wide black and teal leather belts angled low on her hips, then moved upward again to the shining, wheat-colored hair skimming her shoulders. "Very," he returned finally, indicating the room behind him with a desultory nod. "They're waiting for you."

Eden had been hoping for a little of the polite indifference with which he'd treated her before. The polite part was there, but the look in his eyes was anything but indifferent. Telling herself to be grateful for what she could get, she turned toward the open doors. Cables for the TV cameras stretched across the floor, the technicians working around a half dozen reporters gathered by the chairs in front of a long, cloth-draped table. The microphones had already been set up. "I don't see your men anywhere."

"They're around."

Of course they are, she thought. Eden knew it was their job to blend in or stay on the outskirts quietly watching for any signs of disruption. All she was trying to do was keep up some pretext at casual conversation.

Since Matt had dead-ended that topic, she opted for another. "I stopped by Niki's room to make sure he was ready. His manager said he'd be right down. Have you seen him?"

"I have," he returned, quashing a self-deprecating smile when his minimized response caused her soft brown eyebrows to pinch in exasperation.

It would seem that he'd misjudged her. He'd fully expected her to ignore him this morning. Or at least give some indication that she hadn't been too pleased with the way things had ended between them last night. Instead, she was trying very hard to treat him as she did everyone else. He'd noticed that about her before; she had a way of dismissing unpleasantness and going on as if nothing had happened. But other than that—and the way she'd looked in that wet gown—he hadn't paid that much attention to her in Italy. The last sixteen hours had been spent making up for that oversight.

"You have?" She'd come straight from Niki's room and he'd still been in it. Therefore, Matt must have seen him earlier. Thinking it would certainly take more than one or two words for him to tell her about that encounter, she looked up at him. "When?"

"Just now," he informed her, his voice lowering a little. "Mr. Dubikov is right behind you."

If Eden had been paying as much attention to what was going on around her as she was to the shaving nick in Matt's nicely molded jaw, she'd have noticed the four people patiently waiting for her to end her conversation. Since she didn't seem to be making much progress with that conversation, she supposed she might as well give up for now. He was clearly more concerned with getting everyone inside than with her attempt to be nice.

Matt finally allowed the smile he'd suppressed to surface when she tipped her chin and walked away, only to con-

sciously flatten it when, a few moments later, Dom caught
him watching Dubikov hold out a chair for Eden as they
settled themselves behind the microphones. It was easy
enough to see from the way the violinist was treating her that
he'd already succumbed to her considerable charm. No
sense letting Dom see that she was beginning to get to him,
too.

"I'll stay out here if you want to go inside," he heard
Dom offer as Eden turned a calm, professional smile to
people milling about the room. From where he and Dom
stood in the doorway, they heard her ask the reporters to
take their seats. A moment later, an anticipatory silence fell
over the group. "I don't know what you've been so concerned about. It looks to me like she knows what she's
doing."

There was the slightest hint of censure in Dom's observation. It was accompanied by the narrowing of his sharp
brown eyes that clearly couldn't see why Matt was so uptight
about having Eden around.

"Appearances can be deceiving. You know that."

"I also know that some things can be taken at face
value."

"Like her?" Matt inquired, nodding toward the woman
who'd just finished introducing Dubikov to the members of
the press.

"Like her," Dom repeated, tossing his empty plastic coffee cup into the trash can by the double doors. "You're in
charge of this operation, Matt. But for whatever it's worth,
Steve and I both thought you were kind of rough on her
yesterday. Don't you think you could let up on her a little?"

Wondering what the agent would do if he felt things were
slipping out of control, Matt muttered, "I'm working on
it," and jammed his hand into his pocket.

Control, to Matt, meant rules. Eden had said she didn't break them. She only bent them a little. Considering the kinds of things that could happen when she did that, he was more inclined than ever to see the wisdom of keeping to certain mandates—such as the one he'd imposed on himself about never getting involved with someone he worked with. Gossip had a tendency to fly thick and fast in the circles in which he and Eden moved, and his private life was something he'd learned to keep to himself. The less people knew, the less they had to use against you.

Knowing everything you could about someone else, though, provided definite advantages. Matt always preferred to have the advantage. With Eden he had the feeling he'd be wise to maintain that edge.

Vaguely aware that Dom had muttered something, he jerked his head to the side. "Ah . . . what did you say?"

"I said," Dom patiently repeated, his somber expression melting into a knowing grin, "that you shouldn't spend too much time trying to work it out. If the woman's getting to you the way I think she is, you'll probably just wind up with a headache."

"What do you mean?"

"Never mind," Dom chuckled, apparently sensing that Matt wasn't really listening. Pulling the first door closed, he glanced over his shoulder. "You going in?"

Frowning, Matt mumbled, "Yeah," and slipped into the room as the second door closed soundlessly behind him. A lot could be learned through observation, and Matt had a feeling that if he was going to stay one step ahead of Eden, he'd better learn everything he could about her. Just since yesterday he'd discovered the open curiosity she expressed about people, and a kind of genuine thoughtfulness that he hadn't thought existed anymore. Then there was that appealing innocence, something he found a little surprising in

a woman who'd seen as much of the world as she had. She
was thoughtful and caring and...

...Capable of causing heaven only knew what kind of
trouble, Matt firmly reminded himself, watching her talk
with Dubikov and Androvich after the conference was over.
Seeing Eden's smile falter when he caught her eye, he ignored the slightly unpleasant sensation her reaction caused
and tried to decide which one of them—Eden or Dubikov—he needed to watch more closely.

For the better part of the day, Eden had been aware of the
way Matt's eyes followed her. Something about being under his constant surveillance made carrying on an intelligent conversation in Russian more difficult than it should
have been. By five o'clock that afternoon, though, she
wasn't blaming her inarticulateness on Matt's distracting
presence. He was there in the concert hall, all right. Somewhere, just like the rest of his men and Niki's companions.
She had yet to figure out why everyone was keeping such a
close eye on the poor man. It was easy to understand why
they'd want to protect him from his fans, but everyone
treated him like he was going to vanish into thin air.

Niki's constant guard wasn't her concern at the moment.
What was causing her struggle for words was the musician's rapid-fire explanations and the effort it took to
transform the obscure musical terms he used from Russian
into English. She stood onstage between Niki and Bernard
Lenstrom, the lanky, white-haired conductor of the Boston
Symphony. Seated behind them were the musicians of the
orchestra.

"Mr. Dubikov wants a slight arpeggio leading into the
third movement. He says that will create the excitement he
wants to begin his second solo. He also adds that he most
respectfully hopes you agree."

The conductor pushed a cloud of white hair from his face as he headed back to his podium. "Thank you, Ms. Michaels." Raising his baton, he nodded at Niki. Niki, smiling through his beard at Eden, repositioned a linen handkerchief between his chin and his Stradivarius.

The cry of flutes accompanied Eden back to her seat in the sixth row. For over three hours now, she'd been calling her translations out from there, or running up to the stage when it looked like more than a few words needed to be exchanged. Tomorrow, she reminded herself for the third time, she'd wear lower heels. If tennis shoes didn't look so tacky with dresses, she might have considered wearing a pair.

"Aren't they getting along?"

Over her shoulder, she saw Matt standing directly behind her, his hand curved over her seat back. She'd been so preoccupied that she hadn't even noticed his approach.

"As well as can be expected," she returned, softening her sigh with a smile as she crossed her legs to wedge sideways in the seat. While Niki and Mr. Lenstrom had the utmost respect for each other, they were both somewhat temperamental. That had quickly become apparent during their luncheon. "Any time you get two strong-willed people together, you're bound to have differences of opinion."

"We seem to have a few of those ourselves, don't we?"

There was no inquiry in his tone, only the flatness of conviction. "A few," she agreed, determined to keep the promise she'd made to herself. "There's nothing wrong with that, though. Life would be rather dull if we all thought the same way."

The little lines around his eyes crinkled at the corners when he smiled. "I think I'm willing to settle for dull."

Not at all sure why something as ordinary as a smile should make her heart echo the beat of the kettledrum on stage, she watched him take the seat just behind her and to her left. "Are you calling a truce?"

"Are we at war?"

"I was beginning to think so."

"Why?"

For a moment, she thought he was serious. But just as she was thinking that he couldn't possibly be that dense, he gave her a smile that was both disarming and downright sexy. He knew quite well that their beginnings had been less than auspicious.

The silver in his hair glinting, he nodded to indicate the performers on stage. "How many times are they going to go over that piece?"

"Until they get it right," she replied, fully appreciating his diplomatic change of subject. "I think Mr. Lenstrom is having a little trouble getting used to Niki's style."

Leaning forward when she glanced toward the stage, Matt mumbled, "I can sympathize." Mr. Lenstrom wasn't the only one who found someone's way of doing things difficult to understand. Matt didn't have the slightest clue as to how that puzzling mind of Eden's worked, but he was going to find out. If he couldn't understand her, then predicting her would be impossible. "Mind telling me why you took a job with the State department?" he asked, wondering if she knew how provocative she looked sitting at that particular angle.

With the top buttons of her dress left open, he could glimpse the tiniest bit of pale-blue lace against the soft swell of her breast. Two tiny freckles met the edge of that lace. He couldn't quite help speculating about how many more were hidden beneath that filmy covering.

"I don't mind," he heard her reply when her head turned back toward him. "My job at the UN didn't allow me to travel, and this one does. A year of being stuck in a translation booth was about all I could take.''

Thinking it best to forget about the freckles for now, he eyed her evenly. ''Travel is important to you?''

''I think it's more like necessary,'' she returned with a little half laugh that did something rather incredible to the nerves along the base of his spine. ''I grew up just about everywhere, and I guess that kind of moving around got in my blood. Why do you do it?''

With practiced ease, he dismissed her question with nothing more responsive than a shrug and a vague ''Why not?''

''That's not a reason,'' she chided gently.

''Do you have a reason for everything you do?''

He wasn't particularly surprised with her quiet ''No.'' He did, however, find it rather interesting that she'd so freely admit to that lack of rationality. Wondering what other deficiencies were contained in that beautiful head of hers, he delved a little deeper. Maybe the key to her thinking lay somewhere in the unstable past her parents had provided.

Matt knew from her dossier that her father worked for a company with offices in Europe and North America. He also knew she'd been educated in Switzerland, France and England. But when he asked her if she'd found it difficult to make the transitions from one country to another, she simply said, ''Sometimes,'' and proceeded to tell him about a vagabond childhood that seemed so confusing that he had to stop her every other sentence to keep the cast of characters straight.

''Your first governess was the Italian woman?'' he asked, wondering where he'd ever gotten the idea that he'd have to dig to get her to open up.

Pushing her hair behind her ears, she shook her head. ''The first one,'' she reiterated, her eyes alight with the

warmth of memories, "was Aimée. She was French. Sophia was the third, the one in Italy who taught me Spanish."

"Okay. Let's see if I've got this." Folding his hand into a
fist, he let his index finger spring up. "Aimée was first, and
she got you started with your French. The one in England
was Dorothy. She was also your first piano teacher. Next,"
he added, along with another finger, "was Sophia, the one
who spoke Italian and taught you Spanish." At Eden's encouraging nod, he frowned at his fingers. "Leta was Spain
and the one with the horses. That's only four."

"You forgot Mary. She wasn't really a governess, though.
By the time I was fourteen, Mom and Dad were calling them
'companions.' Mary was kind of dull. She did needle-
point."

"So how did you learn to speak Russian?"

"I started with those self-training records, then took
courses after school from an émigré in Switzerland. Eventually I studied it in college and made several trips to the
Soviet Union on a university exchange program."

"Why Russian?"

"Because it was a challenge, I guess. All the other lan-
guages were kind of like music. There was a certain melody
to them. Russian's like German. Kind of guttural, and I
couldn't pick up the tune that easily. I just wanted to see if
I could do it. That's why I'm studying German now," she
went on easily. "But I think I'm going to have to spend some
time along the Rhine before I get it."

"You plan on going to Germany?"

"Someday...if I can talk the department into it."

"Back to travel again, huh?"

Matt couldn't believe how easy it was for her to open up,
to share herself without appearing to suspect his motives at
all. By the time she admitted that the thought of putting

down roots sounded fairly dull to her, he wasn't at all certain what his motive was. Sitting there, intent on hearing the low, cultured tones of her voice over the magnificent melody filling the cavernous space, he was aware of little beyond the effect of her soft smile and the way her slender fingers curved when she lifted her hand to give emphasis to her words. There was such life in her green eyes, and pleasure in their animated depths. It had been a long time since Matt had seen that kind of vibrancy, and something about its freshness appealed to his hardened senses.

"It's time to move on when you stop noticing the buildings you pass, or what kind of flowers are growing along the road," she continued, as if, somehow, she knew he'd never taken the time to look beyond the surface of his surroundings. His powers of observation, acute as they were, limited themselves to what was lurking in shadows. "There's too much of the world to see to limit yourself to what you aren't appreciating."

"Don't you want a home? Kids?" he cut in, a little surprised to hear himself challenging her with such questions. Those were things he rarely thought about, but for a woman like Eden, someone with that built-in ability to give and share, he'd have thought hearth and home would be quite significant.

The look she shot him clearly indicated he'd missed some vital point, then that wonderfully warm smile appeared again. "Home can be anywhere you want it to be. And, yes, I most definitely want a family someday. Travel is a great education for children. My parents raised me that way, and I don't think I turned out so bad."

Several minutes before, Matt had moved forward to rest his elbow on the back of the seat beside her, his head propped in his hand. Now, Eden could quite clearly see the amusement slipping into his expression.

"In some respects," he began blandly, something a little less innocent darkening his eyes as they roamed from the base of her neck to where her dress touched the top of her knee, "I'm inclined to agree."

The crash of cymbals coincided roughly with the sudden leap of her pulse. The phenomenon repeated itself an instant later when Matt's gaze settled on her mouth. "Most definitely," he added, then slid back in his seat and propped his ankle on his opposite knee. "I think you're wanted on-stage."

Though she'd been talking most of the time, Eden had spent the last half hour trying to figure out what it was about this man that she found so compelling. She'd answered every question he'd asked her, but he'd neatly evaded, avoided or shrugged off every one she'd asked him about himself. Now, seeing his bland smile only seconds after he'd visually disrobed her, and still feeling the heady effects of the sensual pull between them, she was even more intrigued.

"Ms. Michaels?" a faintly weary voice called from the podium. The perfect acoustics picked up the maestro's impatience. "May we trouble you again?"

Matt didn't look up until Eden was several feet away. Watching her butterscotch hair bounce while she hurried up the steps, he sat there contemplating the vivacious creature on stage as he slumped down in his seat. Without even being aware of it, his hand had found its way into his pocket, his forefinger and thumb absently rubbing a quarter.

Four

"Mind if I sit here?"

Abandoning her survey of the disappearing lights of Boston, Eden looked up from the small oval window. Matt stood in the aisle of the sleek State Department jet, loosening the knot in his tie. He'd already taken off his jacket and shoulder holster and unbuttoned his vest.

She couldn't resist. "Afraid I'll make the plane take a wrong turn?"

He did his best to suppress a smile. "I don't believe in taking chances. Move over."

"I don't know how you put up with him," Dom said, coming up behind Matt and drawing his attention from Eden's legs as she unfolded them from the plush upholstered seat.

"Just one of those crosses I bear," she returned, sighing.

Matt pretended not to hear her. "Did you want something, Dom? I'm kind of busy here."

"Oh, yeah?" Looking very much like he was about to become privy to some great male secret, Dom's bushy black eyebrows jerked up. "How's that?"

"I'm busy making her life miserable."

"I'm sure you're succeeding admirably." At the level look Matt shot him, Dom's dark features split in an unforgiving grin. Then, sobering just enough to reveal the reason he'd followed Matt to the back of the plane, he added, "The pilot said it's snowing in New York."

Matt's reply was nothing more than a droll "Wonderful."

"That's terrific!" was Eden's own comment, but the quick smile brightening her face crumpled within seconds. Both men were looking at her as if she were slightly daft. "Well, it is," she defended, crossing her arms over the buttons of her sapphire-blue blouse. "New York's beautiful when it snows."

Matt eyed her dully, but it was Dom who spoke. "I'm afraid there's nothing beautiful about traffic jams or delayed flights."

Matt mumbled, "I think we should ignore her," and lowered himself into his chosen seat. Crossing his arms, he stretched his legs out under the seat in front of him.

"Probably so." Dom nodded gravely. "She's the one who told us the caviar and *blini* they served at the reception this afternoon were 'marvelous.' I guess it wasn't too bad," he went on with some reluctance, "if you like that kind of thing. I understand it's an acquired taste."

"Don't be kind," came the admonishment from her right. "More than likely, it was awful."

Eden slanted a slightly mystified glance toward the man occupying the other half of her seat. Sometime during the past few days, Matt had apparently decided it was easier to join forces than oppose them. Like Dom and Steve, he seemed to enjoy teasing her, but there was an indefinable difference in Matt's little gibes, almost a testing quality, something she preferred to overlook in favor of gratitude for the effect it had on his attitude toward her.

Doing her best not to smile, she adopted an expression of prim exasperation. The pleasure in her eyes completely ruined the intended effect. "That's gratitude for you. I sneaked you beluga caviar, and you," she accused Matt, "didn't even taste it. How can you say it was awful?"

She half expected him to pick up on what she really hadn't meant to mention. Security agents weren't regarded as guests at official functions. Because of that, they weren't included in things like buffet lines. Knowing that Matt, his men, and Ivan and Boris, Niki's personal guards, hadn't had a thing to eat since breakfast, she'd filched a few canapés for surreptitious distribution. Ivan's appetite for the imported delicacy had matched Steve's for the crab puffs. Matt, after reproachfully reminding her that she wasn't supposed to do this, had made short work of half a dozen escargots.

He apparently realized that, having devoured the contraband, he was in no position to accuse her. "I've had it before."

"Maybe you'd have liked it this time."

"Eden," he drawled, watching the light shimmering in her eyes. "I find it aesthetically unappealing to eat something that hasn't hatched yet."

"You ate the stuffed eggs."

"That," he evaded, "has nothing to do with snow. Which," he pointed out when he noticed the speculative way Dom's glance kept darting between him and Eden, "is what we were talking about."

"Niki and I were talking about that, too. Just this morning," she mentioned, recalling one of their numerous conversations. Ever since she'd told Niki that she'd studied his music in France, he'd shown an obvious preference for her company. Not that Eden minded. She thought he was one of the nicest people she'd ever met. "He said it's always snowing in Moscow this time of year, so he should feel right at home in New York."

"He looks pretty comfortable right now." Dom stretched, offering the observation over a yawn. "And that's what I'm going to do, too—get comfortable and get some sleep. I know it's a short flight, but I'm beat. Steve's already sacked out, and it looks like everyone else isn't too far behind." Glancing toward the front of the plane, he squinted at the long rows of recessed lights. "Think I'll ask the pilot to turn those out. You mind?"

"Go ahead," Matt said, then moments later as the lights dimmed, he turned to Eden. "How come you're sitting clear back here?"

"Everybody seemed pretty tired when we took off," she answered, matching his quiet tone. The high seat backs seemed to close them in on the snug little space, the low lights demanding equally low voices. "And since I'm not, I thought I'd read. I didn't want to disturb everyone else."

"You want your reading light on?"

She shook her head. "It's okay. I'd rather talk."

"Me, too," he returned, recrossing his arms. "There aren't any changes in the New York agenda, are there?"

Telling herself it was silly to feel disappointed because he wanted to discuss business, she studied the back of the seat in front of her. The jet was very similar to a commercial airliner, and an emergency evacuation guide sat sideways in the magazine pocket. "It's still the same," she assured him, knowing he was referring to the call she'd placed earlier to Barbara to confirm the details. "I would have told you if there were."

"Just checking," he told her agreeably. "I'm only trying to make sure everything goes all right."

"Don't you think things went well in Boston?"

He smiled in a way that only succeeded in conjuring up the images she preferred not to dwell on. Ever since that little episode at the hotel following their limo's encounter with the Volkswagen, that night when she'd thought he'd been about to kiss her, a strange sort of tension had existed between them, a disturbing kind of pull Matt seemed to ignore completely. "All things considered, I suppose they did."

He had the most incredible smile. It was more of a half smile really, almost reluctant. Yet, it did the most marvelous things to his face. She thought about telling him he should smile more often, but settled for another comment on the topic she'd raised.

"All things considered," she echoed, refusing to dwell on his implications, "Boston was a huge success. I know Niki thinks so." Four sell-out performances and the crowd at the reception after his matinee this afternoon attested to that. But Eden wasn't thinking about Niki's pleased reaction. She was wondering if Matt was even aware of the way his eyes strayed to her mouth as they spoke. She didn't mind the way that made her feel, the way he made her feel. She just wished he'd do something besides look at her as if he were ready to devour her at any given moment.

"You and Dubikov seem to be getting along pretty well."

"We are," she returned, but her thoughts strayed right back to Matt.

"I take it he's been behaving himself?"

At Matt's deceptively casual inquiry, Eden stopped toying with the emerald stud in her ear. Matt had been anything but subtle when he'd implied that Niki might try to make a move on her. He'd also been annoyingly certain that she'd allow herself to be taken in by that famous Dubikov charm. "He doesn't have much choice. His manager doesn't leave his side for a second."

"Meaning he wouldn't be acting like such a gentleman if Androvich weren't around?"

For one totally irrational moment, Eden considered responding with nothing more than a shrug. If it had been her nature to be coy, she might have done just that. "I'm sure he'd be every inch a gentleman even if he weren't being watched every single second. You know, Matt," she continued, wishing there was some way she could get through that thick head of his, "if you'd believe what I tell you, you'd have a lot less to worry about. I told you before, I'm not his type. And if it'll help you forget about this, he's not my type, either. I've never cared for men who are that well-polished."

"What kind of men do you like?"

His question threw her a little. The first thing that popped into her head was "the strong, silent kind." "Ones who aren't afraid they'll get too close."

Her remark apparently hit home. Though he sounded very much as if he were simply defending the male half of the population, she saw a tiny frown cross his forehead. "Sometimes a man has his reasons for not wanting to do that."

"Like what?" she ventured.

Several seconds of silence passed. In those seconds the atmosphere underwent a subtle, indefinable change. Maybe it was the nearly imperceptible way he'd stiffened and his conscious effort to counter that reaction that was responsible for the difference. Or maybe it was because, at that moment, she felt she was about to discover something that would be very important to her.

He leaned forward, and turning his head toward her, he quietly said, "Instinct."

All Eden could do was look at him as she tried to comprehend. But it was more than his vague response she didn't quite understand. There was hesitation in his eyes, something that didn't quite fit with the incredible sense of command he exuded. Was it possible, she wondered, feeling the powerful pull of his gaze as it swept over her, that he really wasn't as sure of himself as he seemed to be?

In the dim light and with nothing but the constant hum of the jet's engines to mar the silence, he held her eyes as he shifted to face her. "Instinct, Eden." He repeated the word as if, somehow, he knew she didn't quite understand it. Slowly lifting his hand, the motion as cautious as it was certain, he brushed the tips of his fingers over her cheek. "That feeling you've got to trust because it's seldom wrong. The thing that's telling me to leave well enough alone. But," he added with a reluctant smile, "I don't think I can."

His touch was so tentative she could feel each tiny, invisible hair on her skin as he carried that devastatingly gentle caress toward her temple. Swallowing, she felt her throat constrict. "Why not?"

"Because of all the times I've wanted to do this," he whispered, his palm fitting itself to her jaw as his head inched lower. "Because of all the times I've seen you look at me the way you're doing right now. And if you don't pull back..."

There was no doubt in Eden's mind as to what was about to happen. His unfinished warning still ringing in her ears, she barely had a chance to realize that he wasn't giving her a chance at all before his lips brushed the corner of her mouth. The contact was so brief that she had only the impression of fleeting warmth before he repeated the incredibly light caress.

He was teasing, giving her only the promise of his kiss. She still had a choice, but only he knew that. Feeling the gentle strength of his hands cupping her face, the heat he caused to radiate through her with that simple, undemanding touch, she answered him with a sigh. This was what she'd been hoping for.

Eden didn't know which one of them moved closer. She was aware only of the moan coming from deep within his chest when his mouth closed over hers and the frantic beat of her heart as his arm slipped behind her back. He drew her to him, his hand framing her face as if it were something terribly fragile. His lips felt soft and firm; the nighttime shadow of his beard was tantalizingly abrasive against her skin.

Contrasts. She loved the contrasts. The power he couldn't hide, the tenderness she'd never really suspected. This was the Matt she wanted to know. But mostly she simply felt, absorbed him as one did the air they breathed.

Her hands rested on the smooth wool of his vest. Letting them slip along his shoulders, she was aware of the subtle shift of hard muscle. Briefly, he touched her chin, coaxing her mouth to open. And then, the heady heat of him filled her.

The jolt to her senses was unexpected, far more extraordinary than anything she'd ever experienced before. Testing, seeking, he silently urged her to match the agonizingly slow exploration he had so skillfully begun.

Stars. She'd never before experienced the phenomenon of actually seeing them, but that's what seemed to explode behind her eyelids when the taste of him mingled with her breath. Stars filled a universe that suddenly lacked any substance. All that felt tangible was the man she clung to. There was gentleness in his solid strength, a gentleness she savored. But it was the strength compelling her touch. Her fingers fluttered over his collar, then pushed upward into his hair. Tactile senses joined less definable ones; the crisp feel of the strands curling over her fingers, the hardness of his chest pressed against her.

Rules. There were penalties for breaking them. But the consequences Matt suffered were agonizing enough without worrying about the repercussions of involving himself with Eden. Like a match set to dry tinder, the heat of desire sparked, then flashed through him more swiftly than he'd ever imagined possible. He was a civilized male, a man fully aware of the necessary restraints one placed on oneself to curb the dictates of animal instinct. But the ache centered in his loins threatened that inbred logic. Within an instant of feeling her yield to him, he'd abandoned any attempt at rationalizing his actions. All he was capable of doing was holding back enough to keep from scaring her.

He had no idea where he'd gotten the idea that a simple kiss would satisfy his curiosity about how her lips would taste. With their softness pressed so willingly to his, he knew only that he wanted her. God help him, he thought, forcibly maintaining his control when he heard a dull thud from somewhere ahead of them, he wanted her.

His palm slipped down her throat, coming to rest at the side of her breast. His hand flexed and Eden's breath caught when he seemed about to move it upward. But he let it remain there while his lips caressed her cheek, the corner of her eyebrow, her temple. "Eden," he said, his voice so husky she could barely hear it over the pounding in her ears, "take a deep breath and sit back."

Even before he pulled his hands away, he'd straightened in his seat. Bewildered as much by her scrambled senses as his sudden withdrawal, she watched him smooth her collar. Taking her by the shoulders when she didn't move, he pushed her back in her seat himself. He gave her what was nearly a grin and running his knuckles down her cheek, gently told her, "Someone's coming."

The overhead lights came on just then. "I thought you'd fallen asleep back here," Dom said, looking a little bleary-eyed as he propped himself against the side of the seat in front of them. "The copilot just told me we'll be landing in about ten minutes. So I'm waking everyone up. You want to radio ahead?"

Brushing at the crease in his pants, the motion a study in nonchalance, Matt quite calmly said, "Yeah, I'd better. What's the name of the limo service we're using in New York?"

The question had been directed at Eden, who was doing her level best to appear as nonplussed as Matt seemed to be. She was feeling a little like she had the time her mom caught her necking with Eddie Mayfield in the front seat of his newly acquired Austin.

"Abernathey's," she returned, amazed that she could recall the information while descending from thirty-thousand feet after being kissed completely senseless. A smile touched her lips when she realized that the plane was slowly descending from roughly that same altitude, too.

"I'll be up in a minute," Matt told Dom.

Stretching, Dom sauntered off down the aisle, as Matt had obviously intended, totally oblivious to what he'd just interrupted.

"You'd better straighten your tie," Eden said, blinking over at Matt with all the innocence she could muster. "Heaven forbid someone should guess how it got so crooked."

If it hadn't been for the laughter in her eyes, Matt might have thought she'd taken offense at the way he'd pushed her back so quickly. But there was nothing but amusement in the curve of her kiss-swollen lips. "We'll discuss this later," he informed her, fighting the urge to take one last taste of her mouth. "But for now, I think it's sufficient to say this isn't anyone's business but ours."

It wasn't necessary for him to tell her that. She'd already figured out that Matt guarded his privacy as some people do their possessions. But long after he'd followed Dom down the aisle, Eden sat staring out the window, unconsciously twisting her earring and wondering why she felt so unsettled. It wasn't just the effect of his kiss, though its impact had certainly stunned her. Nor was it the surprise she felt at responding to him so without any reserve. More than anything it was a vague sense of inevitability causing that consternation.

At first, she'd thought she wanted only to get along with Matt. Now, she realized she wanted far more than the easy acquaintance she'd achieved. She wanted to *know* him. She wanted to know why, even when he traded good-natured gibes with his men, he kept himself in check. Why he never seemed to really relax, even on those rare occasions when there were no demands on him. What was it that made him so cynical, and what had happened to make him lose faith in people? That's what bothered her the most, his basic lack of trust. Was that doubt so firmly ingrained in him that it extended to his personal relationships, too?

The answers to those questions might come with time—if Matt would let her get close enough to discover them. That was the problem. If he'd let her get close enough. She wasn't at all sure why that was so important.

Eden had said it was fantastic. As far as Matt was concerned, snow was snow. It was white and cold and wet and made simple things like getting from one place to another more difficult than they needed to be. Eden delighted in the powdery stuff. For the next two days, she brushed off the minor inconveniences it posed as easily as she'd seemed to accept the kiss that had left him more shaken than he cared to admit. He knew he hadn't just imagined her response to him. He'd felt her body yield to his, seen the desire glistening in her eyes when he'd pushed her back. Yet, she was doing nothing to let him know she wanted more. Not, he supposed, that there was anything she could do with a minimum of five other people constantly around. There wasn't much he could do, for that matter.

"What's on the itinerary for tomorrow?" he asked her, frowning as Steve took her arm to lead her around the half-melted puddles in front of the hotel.

"Besides a rehearsal, a luncheon and the obligatory conference with the local press, you mean?" Sliding into the limousine, she brushed the flakes from the front of her coat, reiterating the agenda that called for a visit to the refurbished Statue of Liberty, and translating everything she was saying for Dubikov's benefit.

There was no hope of being alone with her there. Neither was there when they toured an art museum where she obviously enjoyed the nonsensical abstract art as much as the burly violinist did. Matt preferred the type of painting or sculpture that looked like something at least vaguely recognizable. Blobs of color and contorted figures were not his idea of art.

When he told Eden that, it didn't come as any great surprise that she regarded the stuff as something just short of genius. "It's not what you see. It's what you see in it," she animatedly explained when she caught him frowning at a fifteen-foot-high lump of stone. "See that swervy thing on the right?"

Matt nodded.

"That's an arm. And that sort of sweeping thing on top of it is the other one."

"The other one what?"

"The other arm," she said with a low, lilting laugh. "Can't you see it?"

"I guess not," he admitted, not at all sure why he was actually enjoying the impromptu art lesson. He'd found himself enjoying some of the strangest things lately, such as the ice-cream cones Eden had wanted to stop for yesterday when it had been snowing so hard you could barely see.

"You have to use your imagination."

Concentrating on the enticing curve of her mouth, he flatly replied, "I am," and was rewarded with the ill-concealed awareness in her eyes. He was definitely using his imagination. And the images it conjured up had some rather uncomfortable physical effects. He wanted her. In bed. But for now, he'd settle for even five minutes alone with her. Five lousy minutes.

That opportunity finally presented itself the night before they were to leave for Philadelphia. Niki had been tucked in for the night, the last of his performances here having been a sellout like all the others. Steve and Dom had gone down to grab a bite to eat since Eden had been kept too busy at the orchestra's party to filch any food for them. And Matt, having purchased a can of shaving cream from the hotel's gift ship, was riding the elevator back up to their floor, wondering what Eden would do if he showed up at her door.

Eden wasn't in her room. She was standing under one of the ostentatious crystal chandeliers hanging above the row of elevators, wondering where Matt had gone. It had been four days since those few mind-distorting moments in his arms. Four days of trying to keep her knees from buckling every time he looked at her. And four nights of wondering if Matt, Mr. By-the-Book himself, had decided to take his own advice and leave well enough alone.

Not, she thought, hearing the chime when the floor indicator blinked on, that there wasn't some wisdom to that kind of thinking. A man like Matt could absorb a woman, consume her completely. Heaven only knew that he already occupied far too many of her thoughts.

The elevator doors slid open, and Eden's heart promptly slid up to her throat.

She saw Matt's startled expression as he stood there staring at her. It looked very much as if her presence had caught him as unprepared as she was. Finally, his hand shot out to catch the doors as they started to close. Eden hadn't moved. Neither had he.

"Hi," she offered, for lack of anything better to say.

"Hi, yourself," he said, releasing the doors when he stepped out. "Going somewhere?"

"Down to meet Dom and Steve." Crossing her arms over the soft gray wool of her dress, she willed her eyes from his. She didn't think it possible, but what she saw in those unfathomable blue depths actually seemed to be pulling her toward him. Magnetic, she thought inanely, and fought for a countering smile. "Why don't you come with me?"

For one very brief moment she thought he was about to accept her invitation. Then, even before he slowly shook his head, she knew that he wouldn't. Something flashed through his eyes. Something that was a puzzling cross between disappointment and exasperation.

"Thanks. But I'm just going to order room service. Somebody's got to stay up here."

"Why?" she challenged lightly, hoping her own disappointment didn't show. "Nothing's going to happen to Niki. Not with Sergei and Ivan and Boris camped out in his suite."

"All the same," he responded with a little half smile. "I'll pass."

It struck her then, that tendency she'd noticed but never really thought about because circumstances always seemed to excuse it; Matt seemed to deliberately exclude himself from the men's company at times. Neither Steve nor Dom seemed to think anything of it. Whether they were unquestioningly deferring to his instructions or kidding around with him the way they did with her, their respect for him was quite apparent.

So was the overwhelming rush of sensation when Matt reached out to graze her cheek with his knuckles. It was such a simple gesture. Yet, it enlivened every nerve in her body, beginning with those controlling her vocal cords. She'd been about to suggest something, but when he closed the already negligible distance between them, she couldn't remember what it was.

"Did you ever get hold of your mom?"

"My mom?" she whispered.

Nodding, the gaudy chandeliers dropping glints of gold into the silver threading his rich brown hair, he repeated the motion that had paralyzed her voice.

"Oh. Ah . . . yes. A while ago."

"I know you were concerned about not getting through in time."

"It wasn't quite midnight in England, so I just made it."

"Parents are kind of funny about calls on their birthdays."

Wondering why he was smiling at her, Eden wasn't even aware that she'd turned her head into his light caress. "Yours, too?"

"Definitely," he returned, his eyes following the slow motion of his hand. He'd wanted to touch her. That's all, he told himself. Just touch her. "I missed my dad's a few years ago and Mom never let me hear the end of it. The way she went on, you'd have thought I'd disinherited myself. But," he added, with a throaty chuckle, "that's just Mom. Guess the Italian half of her makes her overreact at times."

Matt never failed to surprise her. When she tried to find out something about him, he hedged. But every once in a while, when she least expected it, he'd open up a little.

Liking the way the smoky tones in his voice warmed when he spoke of his parents, but far more aware of the warmth in his touch, she smiled. "Did you forget?"

With the tip of his finger, he traced the gentle shape of her eyebrow, touching what little evidence remained of her encounter with the dashboard. "No. I remembered. There just weren't any phones around."

"She couldn't understand that?"

"She didn't know where I was." His voice more guarded than it had been a moment ago, he muttered, "I suppose I'd better let you go." He contradicted his words by cupping his hands over her shoulders. "In a minute."

Eden moved closer. Whether under her own will or drawn by the silent power of his eyes, she didn't know. Allowing her hand to rest on his lapel, she could feel the strong, steady beat of his heart. "In a minute?" she repeated.

"Yeah. There's something I want to do first."

He was smiling. She knew that because she could feel the upward curve of his lips on hers and she didn't know whether she should be wary or pleased or some jumbled-up combination of both.

She decided to settle for muddled. Because that's what he was doing to her senses. His smile had disappeared, and when she heard him sigh she wasn't sure that he wasn't relieved somehow.

Relief wasn't what Matt was feeling at all. Maybe he had felt it for one fraction of a second when he'd realized she wasn't going to pull away. But what he felt now was nothing so harmless. The instant her mouth had softened, allowing him to taste her incredible sweetness, he could think only of how much he ached for her. Touching her just wasn't enough.

The feel of her against him, the softness of her breasts flattened against his chest, of her hips as he molded her to him, was nearly painful. Every part of his body seemed to scream out to her, wanting to touch, to explore. He drew his hand up her side, along the gentle curve of her waist to fold his hand over the fullness of her breast straining against him. He grazed his palm over the pebbled hardness of her nipple, nearly groaning when he realized how quickly his touch had made her respond. He wanted her. Oh, sweet heaven, how he wanted her.

Oh, *mon Dieu*, she mentally beseeched. What am I doing? What is he doing to me?

Poles. North and South. Opposites attract. She didn't know where those incongruous thoughts came from. Maybe it was because only a few moments ago, she'd felt his magnetic pull and now she was much too close to counter that invisible current. The way he held her spoke of the same urgency she couldn't deny in herself. It was as if something inside her was reaching out to him, begging him to let her inside. She needed that, ached for it in a way that was almost frightening in its intensity.

"Eden." He drew her back, his eyes dark with possession. "Call down to the coffee shop and tell the guys you've decided to stay here."

She knew what staying here would mean. They could go to her room and not worry about curious eyes or interruptions. Eden wasn't as worldly as some of her friends, but she wasn't inexperienced. And from the demands her body was making on her, she knew that cautious caresses and quiet conversation wouldn't satisfy either of them. But never in her life had she been so tempted. "Matt, I..."

He placed a silencing finger over her lips. "I want you, Eden." Slowly withdrawing his hand, he let it rest at the base of her throat. "I want you."

The tug-of-war going on in her brain had to be visible. For long seconds, Matt stared down at her, the raw desire in his eyes and the urgent yearnings of her body pulling her one way, the silent warnings shrieking in her head pulling her the other.

She stepped back, knowing any decision she made would be more reasonable if he wasn't touching her.

The decision was made for her. The ping of the elevator bell was followed by the electronic hum of opening doors. Dom, shaking his head at her, leaned against one side and politely inquired, "What happened to you? Steve's down there alone with a whole order of fried zucchini, and if we don't hurry up, there won't be any left." His brow creasing a little when she didn't move, he looked at the man beside her. "Hey, Matt. You haven't eaten yet, have you? Why don't you join us?"

With a rueful shake of his head, Matt shoved his hands into his pockets. "Thanks, but some other time. Go on," he said to Eden. "We'll, ah . . . talk later."

When Dom stepped to the side for Eden to enter, his attention drawn to the panel of buttons, Eden felt Matt's lips graze the back of her neck. Stunned, she jerked around. But he was already walking away.

They paid agents to notice what was going on. And Dom, being the good agent he was, obviously had noticed far more than Matt had intended. With his finger still on the button to keep the elevator doors open, he gave her flushed features a discerning glance. "You don't have to come with me, Eden."

"Yes, I do," she replied with a faltering smile and pulled his hand away so the doors could close. "I most definitely do."

Five

―――――

"You most definitely will not!"

At Matt's explosive response to Eden's suggestion, an uncomfortable silence fell over the bright, sunlit executive office, magnifying the tension that had increased steadily for the past half hour. Mr. Thurwell Goodman, the manager of the posh Atlanta hotel, cleared his throat. Dom, standing beside Sergei, and Steve, perched on the arm of the mauve sofa Niki occupied, simultaneously stiffened. Even Ivan and Boris looked a little embarrassed. Obviously, no one quite knew what to make of Matt's sudden agitation. No one but Eden.

Undaunted, she blinked at the man who'd just brought all conversation to a screeching halt. There was no way he could blame her for what was happening, but it was easy enough to see he thought her quite capable of compounding the problem.

"Really, Matt," she chided. "I think a simple 'no' would have sufficed."

At her calm response, Niki went back to sipping the Mimosa Mr. Goodman's slightly star-struck secretary had brought him, and everyone else breathed a collective sigh of relief. Everyone but Matt. He simply stood there, his eyes glittering dangerously as he glared down at Eden.

"He's right, Eden." Steve drew his fingers through what little hair he had, clearly seeing some point she'd apparently missed. "That wouldn't be a very good idea at all."

"I must agree," Sergei added with a deferential nod to Matt. "It is not our purpose to become involved in such matters. It will be best to avoid any association."

Eden pushed her hands into the pockets of her teal-blue suede sheath and contemplated the pattern in the cream and mauve dhurrie rug she was standing on. All she'd wanted to do was have one of the drivers take her back to the civic center so she could find out how much longer the picketers planned on protesting. As he had in the last two cities, Niki had requested to see the place where he'd be performing, and, with Matt's permission, they'd driven past the gleaming glass and concrete structure on their way into downtown Atlanta from the airport. That's when they'd seen the demonstration that was threatening to change all their plans.

Harry wasn't going to like this at all.

And Eden didn't like the way Matt was excusing her to Sergei. "I understand that, Mr. Androvich," he allowed, reverting to a more formal tone. "It's just that there are times when Ms. Michaels forgets what can happen when one fails to exert a little caution. She needs to learn to assess situations before getting involved in them. That skill, I believe, will come with time."

"Youth can be impetuous."

"Not to mention idealistic," Matt muttered, half under his breath.

Sergei almost smiled.

The brief flare of pique Eden felt at Matt's gibe was immediately overridden by her desire to salvage what she could of the present situation. They all shared a desire to avoid any situation that might result in adverse publicity.

Straightening her shoulders, she drew a preparatory breath. Part of her job was to see that no political feathers got ruffled, and this matter had to be handled as delicately as possible. "I concede to you both," she offered with good grace, saving the quelling look she'd intended for Matt for some time when it would do her more good. "But I very much hope," she said to Sergei, "that your government does not take offense at what we saw earlier. Anti-nuclear demonstrations aren't anything extraordinary here. It's just unfortunate that Niki's visit to the city appears to have prompted one."

"On behalf of my government, I accept your apology," Sergei returned in observance of that bit of protocol. "Now, I must share our discussion with my comrades." Excusing himself, he went off to confer with the three men on the far side of the room.

While the discussion Sergei instigated was being carried on in Russian, Matt sat down on the arm of a chair. Mr. Goodman nervously waited behind his huge and unbelievably tidy desk. The man was clearly torn between the desire to save the four-night reservation on his penthouse and three ancillary suites and fear of the disruption demonstrators could cause should they decide to picket his hotel if the Dubikov party stayed.

None of the men paid him the slightest bit of attention. Eden, appreciating how it felt to be left out of things, gave him a small shrug and tried to concentrate on what she was hearing. Being closer to Matt's group, she really couldn't discern much from the other end of the room.

"What do you think?" she heard Matt ask Dom and Steve.

"Well," Dom began. "Even if the cops clear out the demonstrators, there's no guarantee they won't be back. They can be a pretty tenacious bunch."

Steve seemed to agree. "And there's no telling how far one of them would go to get publicity."

"You don't think they'd do anything drastic, do you?"

At Steve's question, Matt shrugged. "I doubt it."

"Expect the unexpected," Dom added. "Stranger things have happened. We can't risk any kind of a hostage situation."

"Hostage situation?" Eden quietly repeated. "From a bunch of anti-nuclear activists? Are you serious?"

All three men turned to her, their identical expressions as bland as they were patient. "We're just exploring possibilities, Eden," Matt explained, a little amused by her disbelief. "And in this instance, the possibility isn't even worth considering."

"But it is in others?"

"You never know." He turned back to his men. "My main concern is with keeping them away from him. I'm not sure we can do that."

Good grief, she silently groaned. If this was the way security agents thought all the time, it was no wonder Matt was such a skeptic.

"You'd better go call Winston," Matt told her a moment later. "Have whoever it is that worked out these arrangements call ahead to Philadelphia and see if they can take us a few days early. The sooner we get Dubikov out of the city, the better."

Niki's manager had the remarkable talent of being able to carry on two conversations at the same time. Even as Ivan said something to a rather disappointed-looking Niki, Eden saw Sergei's head come up. "We agree, Matt Killian."

The decision that had taken the men only seconds to make took Eden the better part of the day to put into effect. After calling Barbara and having the hotel in Philadelphia confirm that they'd be ready, Eden was sure everything would go quite smoothly. The two most important matters—getting the pilot back and arranging for accommodations—took precedence. But three hours later, Eden had discovered that the process of moving everything ahead four days was considerably more complicated than she'd first thought it would be.

Whoever Barbara had spoken with at the hotel had been wrong. Somewhere between Atlanta, Washington, D.C., and Philadelphia, the lines of communication had broken down and the person at the hotel hadn't understood. They would indeed be ready for Mr. Dubikov and his party, but not until Tuesday. That bit of news didn't arrive until they were already in the air.

Since the phone in the cabin had decided to complicate matters by refusing to work, the only other means of contact with the rest of the world was the jet's radio. Stifling a groan when Barbara signed off, Eden glanced up to see Matt enter the cockpit. The air force pilot nodded at him, then went back to fiddling with something above his head.

"Problems?" Matt inquired, giving the knees of his slacks a little pull as he squatted down in front of the small jump seat she was sitting in. With his hands clasped between his knees, he rocked back on his heels, meeting her at eye level.

"Nothing we can't handle," she assured him, wondering where she ever got that idea. At the rate they were going, they might all be sleeping in the streets tonight.

"Can I use that now?" Matt asked, indicating the radio.

Nodding, she lifted her hands to remove the earphones. Matt was quicker than she was. His fingers covered hers, his thumb grazing her cheek in a light, deliberate caress.

"I'll do it," he said, then, carefully removing the instrument from her head, he slipped it over his own. His mouth pinched in concentration, he turned to the digital controls the copilot had operated for her, opening the channel himself. A moment later he was identifying himself to the ground operator and giving the number for a Captain Adams.

Eden knew that the limousines Barbara had reserved were still available. One of the drivers who had been cleared by the department was not. That meant finding someone else through the local authorities. Matt was obviously taking care of that now. He was also doing a pretty fair job of shaking her up. His call didn't take long, but all the time he was talking, he never once took his eyes from hers.

"Need these?"

"Yes," she said quietly, and felt the familiar tug at her midsection when he brushed her hair behind her ear before replacing the headset. He tilted his head to one side, the motion silently asking if he'd positioned the instrument properly, and after seeing her barely perceptible nod, remained right where he was while he waited for her next call to go through.

When it did, and after she'd broken the air-to-ground communication, she relayed what she'd learned. "The hotel can take us, but we can't have the rooms Barb originally reserved. They're being occupied until tomorrow."

That meant the security detail from Washington had to fly out to check over the floor where the new room assignments had been made. Then the floor had to be locked off to everyone except the few members of the staff who'd be allowed to service the rooms.

Again, Matt handled that, and Eden was left with nothing to do but wait for her turn and wonder if the pilot was picking up any strange atmospheric readings inside the cockpit. It was all she could do to keep reminding herself that she and Matt were doing nothing but taking care of business.

The calls Eden made from the small military base where they eventually landed were much easier on her nerves. Relatively speaking. While everyone else was being treated to dinner by the base commander, she was in some lieutenant's office trying to talk some sense into Harry. The picky little things he insisted on were driving her nuts. He steadfastly ignored her assurance that, under the circumstances, Mr. Dubikov would understand if everything wasn't quite perfect. Harry thought otherwise and his opinion prevailed during one of the conference calls between him and Eden and Barbara.

So when Niki was escorted to the hotel eight hours after leaving Atlanta, he entered a suite of rooms filled with flowers from a local florist. There was also a basket of fruit and a chilled bottle of vodka waiting for him along with a telegram extending an official apology for all the inconvenience. When he got into the bedroom he'd also find feather pillows instead of the foam ones he didn't like. Had Eden not been so pressed for time, she might have stayed for the compliments Niki and his manager so freely offered. But as it was, she had to get to her own room and finish the discussion with Barbara their departure from the air base had interrupted.

Fortunately, that call didn't take long, and by the time Eden hung up after hearing that she'd just redeemed herself in Harry's eyes, she was ready to feel proud of herself. The experience might have been rather pleasant had she not felt as if she'd just been pulled through a wringer backward.

Letting out a long, weary sigh, she pulled off her shoes, wriggling her toes against the beige carpet before crossing the room to close the heavy beige drapes. A moment later, the task seeming to take an inordinate amount of energy, she tugged her dress over her head. Rather than hang it up, she left it on the chair by the nightstand, carried her panty hose into the bathroom to be rinsed out later, and dropped her slip and bra on the blue and beige patterned bedspread. After rummaging around in her suitcase, which she decided to unpack in the morning, she pulled on a short nothing of a nightgown she'd picked up in a trendy little lingerie shop in Piccadilly and shoved the case aside. Sometime between now and when room service delivered the dinner she was probably too tired to eat, she'd have to dig out her robe.

All the turmoil of the day suddenly caught up with her. It had begun in New York at six o'clock this morning, taken a detour through Atlanta and now, at nine o'clock that night, had ended, finally, in the city our Founding Fathers had called home.

I wonder if George Washington slept here, she thought, falling back on the king-size bed just as a knock sounded on her door.

With a muttered *Sacre bleu*, she pulled herself right back up, called out, "Just a minute," and scrambled around for the short mint-green robe that went with the gown. Stuffing her arms into the sleeves, she whipped the belt around her waist and hurried to the door. Even as she pulled it open, she was turning to motion toward the table. "You can put it over there."

"Do I look like a bell boy?"

Her eyes widening at the sound of Matt's deep voice, she jerked around. No, he most definitely did not look like someone who politely obeyed anyone's beck and call. Even with the faint smile curving his firmly chiseled mouth, the sheer, masculine power betrayed in his careless stance made it clear that he took orders only when he had to. He was much more apt to give them.

She stepped back, consciously fighting the urge to tighten her robe. It didn't make the slightest bit of sense. She'd opened the door to what she'd thought would be a perfect stranger and her state of dress, or undress, hadn't even occurred to her. Now, seeing Matt standing there, all she could think about was how much thigh her skimpy attire exposed.

He didn't even seem to notice. Stepping inside, he closed the door and leaned against it. "I need to know what time to tell the limo drivers to be here. What's going on tomorrow?"

The sleeves of his white shirt were rolled back, exposing the generous sprinkling of dark hair on his muscular forearms. She watched him push his hands into the pockets of his gray slacks, his thin gold watch flashing as it caught the light from one of the table lamps. The subtly striped tie he'd been wearing earlier was gone, along with his jacket and vest, and he'd loosened the top buttons of his shirt.

Eden wished he hadn't shown up half-dressed. As wonderful as he looked in a suit, he was downright sexy when he abandoned its components.

"Nothing, as far as I know," she mumbled, certain he wasn't interested in anything other than finishing up the day's business. They'd worked together all day, the long hours of planning and rearranging and juggling permeated with a sense of easy cooperation. That's all he seemed to be looking for now, cooperation. More than likely he was just as tired as she was—or had been until his sudden presence had recharged her batteries. "Niki said he'd just like to rest since we're ahead of schedule."

"He doesn't want to leave the hotel?"

"I'm not sure what he wants to do. When I left him he was having Sergei read a chamber of commerce magazine to him. Maybe he'll find something in there he'd like to do. I do know he doesn't want to change the schedule here by meeting with anyone from the symphony or university yet . . . or taking any of the tours we've planned."

"So we basically do nothing for the next three days?"

"You make that sound about as appealing as being stranded in a life raft. What's wrong with doing nothing for a change?"

"It's boring."

"How about 'relaxing'? We've been going nonstop for over a week. A day off might be good for everybody."

Not one to be sidetracked for long, Matt reverted right back to his reason for showing up in her room. "He must want to do *something*."

"Well, I won't know what that something is until he tells me. I can offer suggestions, but that's about all. At least he didn't seem too disappointed about having to cancel Atlanta," she added, finding the single bright spot in the whole crazy day. "In fact, he was pretty philosophical about it." To Eden, Niki seemed pretty philosophical about almost everything. His favorite expression was a slightly fractured version of *C'est la vie*. She liked that, and not just because most of her favorite expressions—most of them socially unacceptable—were also in French. "I think he'd have been a lot more upset if we'd had to cancel San Francisco or Los Angeles.''

Matt raised his eyebrow, indicating more interest than Eden had expected in her offhand observation. ''Why do you say that?''

Her brow furrowed. A couple of days ago, when he'd casually asked if Niki ever mentioned anything about his family, that same expectant look had creased his face. The only time she'd raised the subject, Sergei had answered for Niki. All he'd said was that Niki's parents were retired, then hustled Niki away. She'd told Matt about that in response to his question, but all he'd done was nod and wander off in search of Dom.

''Just the impression I get,'' she returned, remembering all the times Niki had asked her about the various cities on the itinerary. He was naturally curious about all of them, but he seemed most interested in the ones on the West Coast. ''Maybe it's because of all that propaganda California puts out about beaches and tall, tanned, blue-eyed blondes.''

Most men would have at least smiled at her description, but Matt's mumbled ''Could be'' sounded as preoccupied as he looked.

There was no time for Eden to wonder why Matt's mind suddenly seemed to be visiting another planet. The knock on the door had him distractedly motioning the kid from room service inside.

Echoing the instructions she'd given him a minute ago, he told the young man where to put the food and followed him to the table. Eden used the distraction to snatch up the bra and slip she'd left on the bed and hurriedly shoved them into her suitcase while Matt signed the check. What she wore was far more modest than the bikinis she thought nothing of wearing to the beach. But she just didn't have it in her to justify leaving her undergarments lying around with Matt in the room.

Not that he would have noticed, she drawled to herself. When Matt was thinking about work, very little seemed to distract him. It was obvious enough he was thinking about work now. As soon as the young man left, Matt was on the phone, telling whoever was on the other end that he didn't know what their plans were yet, but he'd let them know as soon as possible. He made a second call, but the person he asked to speak with wasn't in, and left her room number for a call back. Then, seconds after he left his message, the phone rang and it was her turn.

"Yes, Harry," she said, trying not to sigh. She turned away from Matt, deliberately telling herself his shoulders weren't all *that* broad, and twisted the cord around her finger. "I promise I'll let you know what he wants to do just as soon as he tells me. Yes, Harry," she repeated, certain Barbara had just made up that remark about how pleased Harry was with her performance today, "I will." With an overly cheerful good-night, she broke the connection. It seemed as if everybody in the western hemisphere wanted to know what Niki was going to do tomorrow.

Matt was sitting on the edge of her bed. Dropping into the chair by the table across from him, she glanced at him wearily. "I swear if I never make or receive another phone call, it'll be too soon. My ear actually hurts."

"I know what you mean. As soon as I get the one I'm waiting for, I think I'm through for the night." He smiled a mysterious little half smile and motioned toward the tray of food beside her. "Eat."

"You think that'll make my ear feel better?"

"Probably not," he drawled, coming over to hand her the glass of white wine she'd ordered to reward herself. "But maybe this will."

Her fingers had barely closed around the goblet when he leaned down to brush his lips against her earlobe. If he hadn't still been hanging on to the glass, she probably would have dropped it. Maybe he knew that because, just before he straightened, a mere two seconds later, he picked up her other hand and placed it at the stem.

"You did a hell of a job today," he remarked casually, wandering over to check out the view behind her drapes. He chuckled, shaking his head. "In fact, I don't think I've ever seen anyone pull something like this off quite as fast as you did. You really surprise me sometimes."

You surprise me, too, she thought, telling herself that a little kiss 'to make it better' was nothing to get excited about. "Thanks. I didn't do it alone, though. Mr. Winston's secretary practically held my hand every step of the way. She'd probably have done it all herself, except she had to cancel everything in Atlanta, too. We just divided up the work."

It was apparent enough that Matt planned on staying until his call came. Since they'd been sharing phones all day, not to mention most of what those calls were about, she really couldn't object. What she did object to was the way her mind kept straying back to what he'd done a moment ago. As in the way he'd brushed the hair from her cheek just before they'd left the cockpit this afternoon, there was a certain familiarity in his gesture. Yet, he'd done nothing else. It was almost as if he didn't trust himself with anything more than a touch.

Quashing thoughts of what she wanted in favor of a little self-distraction, she glanced down at her plate. Maybe it would help if she pretended he were Dom or Steve, she thought. Or that he had two heads. That should keep her mind from wandering.

"Want some fruit?"

The plate of fruit she uncovered was huge, far more than she'd ever be able to eat herself. Though Matt had had dinner, she knew from the hurried lunches she'd had with him and Dom that his appetite was positively enormous. She'd watched him polish off a deli sandwich, two orders of fries and an order of potato salad, then stop for a couple of candy bars half an hour later. If the way he was eyeing her offering was any indication, slices of pineapple, oranges, pears and papaya weren't his idea of a meal.

"No offense," he prefaced, watching her wash down a juicy bite of pear with her wine, "but I've eaten enough fruit to last me a lifetime. About all I can stand are apples."

"Why apples?" she inquired, swallowing back the other questions his comment had raised along with a small slice of papaya.

"Because they didn't grow where I was stationed. If they had, I'd probably have had my fill of them, too—them and fish. Maybe," he added, smiling as he reached for her wine, "that's why I don't like caviar." Watching her over the rim of the glass, he took a small sip and handed the glass back. "Not bad," he pronounced, seemingly very aware of the way her eyes had followed his motions.

Eden slowly tore a section of orange in half. "Where were you stationed?"

"A little place in Central America you've probably never heard of."

"I'm very good at geography," she told him. "Whereabouts in Central America?"

"On the coast," he returned in that maddeningly evasive way of his.

"What were you doing there?" The second half of the orange went the way of the first, and she started tearing at another.

"Something you're surprisingly good at most of the time," he qualified. "Right now, I'd say your technique is terrible."

Totally confused, she blinked at him. Eden had turned her chair to face him when Matt had sat back on the edge of her bed, and his knees almost touched hers. Even that close, though, she couldn't detect a single clue in his expression as to what he was talking about. "My technique?"

"Uh-huh. The way you go about drawing information out of people without them being aware you're doing it."

"Maybe I'm just curious."

"Oh, I don't doubt that. But you know what they say about curiosity."

Eden was as well versed in trite expressions as anyone else. Carrying the one Matt referred to one step further, she pointed out that, "They also say cats have nine lives," and set the orange back down. "How many of those lives have you used?"

It had taken only a few seconds for Eden to figure out what he wasn't quite telling her. He'd been stationed in Central America and his allusion to eating only tropical fruit and fish made it apparent to her that he hadn't been working out of one of the embassies. And when she'd asked what he was doing there, he'd skirted the question, but more or less inferred that he was obtaining information without anyone knowing about it.

"I've probably reached my limit," he admitted, and though his reply was casual enough and he immediately smiled, she knew there were probably several excellent reasons for the cloak of secrecy he'd woven around his past. Or, she wondered, watching him sip her wine, was it still his present?

"Matt?" she ventured carefully, keeping her eyes on her napkin as she wiped the juice from her fingers. "Exactly what kind of work do you do?"

He didn't hesitate, but she could hear the note of displeasure in his voice. "You know what I do."

"Maybe I should phrase it another way." Meeting his eyes as calmly as she could, she quietly asked, "Are you in intelligence?"

A moment ago he'd looked puzzled. Now, he looked at her as if he couldn't quite believe she'd asked him that. "Not anymore," he said, sounding oddly defeated. "How'd you know?"

"I didn't." But now that I do, she thought, things are beginning to make more sense. "What made you quit?"

"Nothing in particular." Shrugging, he added, "Everything in general."

"That's not an answer."

Prodded by the gentle light in her eyes, Matt drew a low breath. "You've traveled a lot, so you know that there's a lot to be seen out there. It just got to the point where I saw too much."

If some of the stories she'd heard about covert operations were true, she wasn't sure she wanted to hear about what he'd witnessed. But he was finally letting her inside, and she'd listen to anything he was willing to tell her. "What did they have you do?"

He tried to smile. The attempt might have been quite successful if it hadn't been for the bleakness she saw dart through his eyes. He didn't want to remember. She was sure of that. Knowing that some things were better left buried, she could have kicked herself for asking that question. The last thing in the world she wanted to do was resurrect unpleasant or painful memories.

"You don't want to know."

No, she thought, she probably didn't. The more she learned about him the more sure of that she became. They shared the same space, but they lived in two very different worlds. And, if she wasn't careful, he could really make a mess out of hers. He'd already done a pretty fair job of tilting its orbit. "Yes, I do. But only if you want to tell me."

For one incredibly long moment, she was afraid he'd want to know why it mattered to her. Since she couldn't answer that question for herself, she certainly couldn't enlighten him. When he didn't ask, she all but held her breath, waiting for the shutter to fall over his eyes and block out what little he was letting her see.

He slowly put the wine on the nightstand and Eden thought he was going to move away. Instead, he leaned forward to fold his fingers through hers. "Eden," he began, watching his thumb trace the delicate veins in the back of her hand. "Even my family doesn't know that. They knew I worked for the government, but they thought I was with the diplomatic corps. I couldn't tell them otherwise for their own protection. I went to work for the department five years ago so I wouldn't have to worry about keeping a cover anymore. Do you understand what I'm saying?"

"I understand," she replied. "I won't ask any more questions."

He lifted his head, his beautifully wry smile telling her just how little faith he had in that statement. "Why don't I believe that?"

"Because you're a born skeptic?" she suggested, hoping her teasing would make him forget something he so obviously hadn't wanted to remember.

"I thought you said I was a cynic."

"When did I say that?" she asked and felt his hands slide up her arms.

"Does it matter?"

The tips of his fingers moved under her sleeves, closing around her upper arms. Gamely, she kept her eyes on his. "No."

He drew her forward, the light of the lamp disappearing as his face blurred in front of her. "Good," he whispered, the heat of his breath feathering over her mouth. "Because when I get this close to you I have a devil of a time remembering much of anything."

She knew exactly what he meant. She couldn't think of anything except how incredibly soft his lips felt as they moved from her ear, to the hollow of her throat. The very gentleness of his touch made it impossible to remember all those wonderful little lectures she'd given herself about how she wasn't going to let him do this to her anymore. How she was going to resist the seductive temptation of his mouth when he coaxed her lips to part. How she wasn't going to respond to the distorting way he had of turning her into jelly with the skilled seduction of his hands.

If he'd demanded at all, she might have been able to fight him. But she couldn't fight when he wasn't exerting any force. "Let me hold you," he whispered softly, the plea in his voice telling her how very much he needed that contact right now. "I just want to hold you." It was a promise of sorts, a quiet assurance that she was in control. That nothing was going to happen unless she wanted it, too.

What little mental resistance she'd mustered slowly melted to compliance. It's okay, she told herself, letting her hands settle on his shoulders. I can pull back anytime I want.

With that rather audacious guarantee trying to override more rational probabilities, she decided that, just for a moment, she wouldn't think at all. She'd simply feel. It was an amazingly easy feat to accomplish, and her first conscious sensation was how hard his chest was when he folded his arms around her back and drew her to him. For long moments, he simply held her, then, after he nudged her cheek to bring her head up, she let his mouth work slowly over hers. Those moments, as achingly sweet as they were, slowly created a desire that threatened to obliterate what little sense she had left. The only reason she'd bothered with the feeble attempts to deny what she knew she wanted was because she didn't want her heart to get in on the act. She should have practiced that denial sooner. It felt very much as if her heart was already involved.

Still holding her close, he drew her down. His weight pressed her back against the mattress, and she felt him tug at the thin belt of her robe. Hot, tender little kisses rained along her neck, over her collarbone, then once more he was seeking her mouth. The palm of his hand slipped under her gown, grazing her stomach before slowly working up to cover her breast. The fire he'd ignited within her felt dangerously close to flaring out of control.

Matt felt the way the hard muscles of her stomach flexed beneath his fingers, her breath catching when he began moving his palm in a slow circle. He knew he was only seconds away from peeling off the tiny scrap of satin she wore and taking off his own clothes. Oranges. He thought he hated them. But tasting their sweetness mingled with the wine in her mouth, he thought the nectar of the gods must surely be made of them. She smelled of powder and felt like silk. And he wanted something far more from her than a few stolen hours in her bed.

Matt felt himself go still. He had to stop while he still could. He'd just realized that making love with Eden wouldn't be enough. It might never be enough.

"Time-out," he said, hearing the huskiness in his own voice as he raised himself to his elbow and pulled her robe together. There were three freckles, only one more than he'd seen before, at the top of her breast.

She stared up at him, her hands against his chest. The look in her eyes was an array of emotions he couldn't begin to figure out, but he couldn't let himself look at her for very long. The one emotion he did recognize was confusion.

"Come here." Taking her by the shoulders, he pulled her up to sit next to him and picked up the nearly empty glass of wine. "You'd better finish this before I do. I owe you half a glass already." When all she did was sit there staring at him, he closed her hand around the glass and stood up. He still had his back to her when he heard the faint tremor in her voice.

"What did I do?"

"It's not you, Eden. It's me. That shouldn't have happened. I'm sorry."

"Matt," she began, bewildered as much by his apology as his abrupt withdrawal. "Why...?"

He touched a finger to her lips, then drew it back to brush the wisps of hair from her forehead. "It's getting kind of late. If a guy named Robertson calls, give him my room number, okay?"

"Okay," she whispered. "But..."

"Eden. Don't. I'll see you in the morning." Bending, he dropped a quick kiss on the tip of her nose and within about three seconds he was gone. The last thing he wanted to do was try to explain something he didn't even understand himself.

Six

Long after Matt left, Eden sat contemplating the goblet she still held in her hands. Prompted by the more rational ponderings that surfaced over her confusion, she took a fortifying gulp of wine.

Just that morning Matt had told Sergei that she needed to assess situations before getting involved, that she failed to consider what can happen when a person fails to exhibit a little caution. It was entirely possible, she admitted to herself, that he was right.

The first time he'd kissed her, she'd been vaguely aware of some strange sense of the inevitable. That nagging premonition had told her exactly what would happen to her if their relationship proceeded on its present course, but she'd done nothing to change its direction. If anything, she'd deliberately ignored the warning signs posted at every curve on that road, and if she didn't slam on the brakes right now, she'd find herself going right over the edge.

Maybe, she thought, twirling the glass in her fingers, that's where the expression "emotional wreck" came from.

Drawing her hand through her hair, she set the goblet aside. It was time to face a few pertinent facts—starting with those she'd encountered before but never really considered.

Every time Matt let his protective guard slip a little, he'd almost immediately start to pull back. She'd noticed that many times, but never had he retreated as far and as obviously as he had tonight. He didn't want the kind of closeness she needed. If anything, he fought it as if the very thought threatened him somehow.

Had he ever allowed himself to become involved in a truly caring relationship? she wondered, then quickly abandoned that thought. There was no doubt in her mind that Matt had quite probably fractured a few hearts on more than one continent. To think he lived the life of a monk took more imagination than even she had. But dwelling on that didn't help at all.

What did help was realizing that what she looked for was the same thing he ran from.

"Add that to your list of differences," she mumbled to the drapes, and hugging her arms around her, set about getting ready for bed. If she went to sleep, she wouldn't have to think.

It was exactly midnight when she came to the decision she should have made days ago—the one that should have been clear as soon as she'd realized how little she and Matt had in common. In many ways, he was a loner. She wanted someone to share experiences with, someone who wasn't afraid to let her care about him. Therefore, for the next two weeks and six days, she'd be the epitome of the caution he didn't think she possessed. And, maybe, since she'd caught herself in time, she wouldn't fall in love with him. Never having been in love before, she didn't think to question her optimism.

Caution was something Eden never thought about with Niki. He'd proved to be one of the kindest, most genuine people she'd ever met. "I'd be delighted," she told him, responding to his invitation to join him in his suite for breakfast.

They'd shared many meals together and this morning, as always, Sergei was there. The conversations Eden and Niki carried on in Russian usually bounced from one subject to another. They discussed music, of course, since they both adored it, and food, because Niki loved to eat. Now, though, the main topic was how he wanted to spend the next few days.

"You don't have to do anything if you don't want to," she told him, adding lemon to the cup of hot tea he'd poured for her. The Russians had the same affinity for tea as the British, only Niki told her that, at home, they drank it from glasses with metal bases and handles. Here they had to settle for china or ceramic cups.

"Then I believe I'll do nothing." Slathering butter over a flaky croissant, he smiled through his neatly trimmed black beard. "In Moscow, when we do nothing we play chess, but what does one do in America?"

"We have games, too," she returned as Sergei, who'd been sitting on the sofa reading the paper all during breakfast, wandered into one of the other rooms. "But I suppose one of the great American pastimes is watching television."

She saw Niki's mouth pinch, his heavy black eyebrows snapping together as if he found little appeal in that form of entertainment. Then, looking very much as if he'd come to some kind of decision, he glanced toward the empty doorway and lowered his voice to a whisper.

"Eden Michaels," he began, his brown eyes serious, "I wish to tell you that I regard you as my friend. A friend to be trusted," he expanded furtively, touching the back of her hand. "Are you?"

Surprised by both the abrupt change in subject and the sense of urgency in his question, she quietly replied, "Of course."

"It is not a matter of course," he countered. "It is not something to be taken for granted. But I feel I can rely upon our friendship, should the opportunity arise."

He started to say something else, but he quickly straightened, grinning a little too broadly when Androvich walked back in with a magazine. "Then I shall keep to my rooms with the television. You will stay and translate for me to save dear Sergei's breath? I will order lunch. A salmon perhaps, or if the chef can properly produce it, a tureen of borscht."

She nodded, acknowledging the strange sadness in his eyes with a softly compassionate smile, and told him she'd love to stay. It hadn't occurred to her that he'd been seeking her because he thought of her as a friend. She felt quite honored to have him bestow that distinction on her, but more than that, she felt sorrow.

It was clear enough that his relationship with Sergei and Ivan and Boris wasn't as comfortable as hers with the men she worked with—two of those men, anyway. And she was beginning to see what Matt had meant when he'd said that lack of trust was something you learned to accept. Niki obviously had. Though he was on a cultural mission for his country, something he took great pride in, Sergei never left his side unless Ivan or Boris was around. Niki was watched constantly. She wished she knew why they didn't trust him, and what Niki had meant by relying on their friendship should the occasion arise.

Directing her thoughtful frown to the television's remote control, Eden judiciously avoided the cable selections of American war movies and tuned in a light, politically inoffensive romantic comedy. One of the more selfish reasons she'd jumped at Niki's request to spend the day watching television with him was because translating a movie would keep her mind off Matt. Not only that, but by staying here, she could avoid him for a while. Before she could start avoiding him, though, she had to advise him of Niki's plans for the day.

"We won't be needing the limos," she told him, clutching the phone a bit more tightly than was necessary. "The agenda consists of television, lunch here, and more television. Tomorrow," she went on, relating what Niki had come up with only moments ago, "he wants to go shopping."

There was a slight pause on the other end of the line. "What are you going to do?"

"Stay here," she quickly returned. "He wants me to translate for him."

"Where's Androvich?"

"With us."

Another brief moment of hesitation followed. "Okay," he said, his tone so flat she couldn't begin to figure out what he was thinking. "Since Dubikov's staying put, I'll tell the guys they can have the day off."

She could have kicked herself for asking, but she did anyway. "What will you do?"

"Take it off with them. We're not leaving the hotel. If you need us, we'll probably be down in the gym. I'll call you when we get back."

"Do you want to order the cars for tomorrow, or should I?"

Matt said he'd take care of it and after she'd given him a time, he broke the connection. An hour later, he appeared at Niki's door. Looking gloriously male in a pair of gray sweats, the front of his shirt dark with a long vee of perspiration, he wiped his face with the hotel towel slung around his neck.

"Dom and I are going to have lunch in the bar. Steve's doing laps." Though it seemed to take a deliberate effort for him to keep his glance from straying over the emerald-green blouse she'd tucked into her tan slacks, his manner was as remote and distant as his voice. "Any change in plans here?"

"No," she assured him, finding it more difficult than she'd have imagined to ignore the odd tension between them. "Everything's still the same." Ivan and Boris were parked in front of the TV now, too.

The cool blue of Matt's eyes darkened slightly when they met hers. Then, he nodded and headed down the hall, apparently feeling there was nothing else to be said.

That's how it went all day. Every couple of hours, he'd either call or stop by, never keeping her for a moment longer than was absolutely necessary. By the time Niki had thanked her for spending the day with him and went to bed at nine o'clock, Eden wasn't so sure that her decision to exert a little caution had even been necessary. It was painfully apparent that Matt was exhibiting enough for both of them.

By the next day, she was ready to forget all about wariness and put an end to the strain of trying to deal with a situation without actually confronting it—which, she told herself as she headed into the hotel's coffee shop, was exactly what she and Matt were doing. Twenty-four hours of talking without communicating was about all she could take.

Her nerves couldn't handle much more, either. Matt was sitting with Dom in one of the pink, semicircular booths. Not quite prepared to see him yet, she felt as if every cell in her body went on red alert. Ordering the ones controlling her legs to keep moving, she issued a similar instruction to those controlling her vocal cords—along with a firm admonishment that they not shake—and plastered a commendably bright smile on her face when she reached their table.

"Is there room for one more?"

Dom was the first to respond. "Only if you don't mind discussing football." Grinning, he slid down on the bench, giving her the place across from Matt. Behind her, the clink of silver against china punctuated quiet conversations. "Did you happen to catch the Chargers/Cowboys game yesterday?"

"We watched a lot of TV," she admitted, propping her elbows on the table as the waitress approached. "Thanks. Just coffee," she said, when the young girl started to hand her a menu. "But I'm afraid we missed that channel."

"Too bad." Dom gave an exaggerated sigh and turned back to his eggs. "Heard there were a couple of great passes. They had another game on in the bar yesterday, so we missed it."

Matt's breakfast was already gone, as was some of the coolness he'd exhibited the last time she'd spoken with him. His manner was quite civil, even if he didn't exactly appear overjoyed to see her.

"Ever play football?" he asked her, setting aside his coffee in favor of his remaining orange juice.

Orange juice? she thought. He'd said he hated oranges. "Sure." Giving the absurd question all the seriousness it was due, she smiled. "I was a quarterback. Used to get that ball over home base all the time."

The corners of Matt's mouth lifted slightly at her deliberate blunder, accentuating the deep, masculine grooves in his cheeks. "Yeah. Me, too."

"He ever tell you about his brush with the big league?"

Blinking at Dom, she blew across her coffee to cool it. "Matt's?"

"Uh-huh." Swallowing a mouthful of toast, he wiped his face with a pale pink napkin. The square of pastel linen was dropped on his plate, and he reached for his cup. "Seems our illustrious leader here had a future with 'em at one time. Amazing what you can learn over a beer in a bar."

Cocking her head to one side, she carefully considered Matt's rather disgruntled expression. That fleeting scowl disappeared in the next instant. "You played professionally?"

Both Matt and Dom, she discovered, had played football in college. Matt, though, had apparently been eyed by one of the pro teams. When he cited lack of confidence as the reason he didn't pursue that career, Eden nearly choked on her coffee. If there was one thing Matt didn't lack, it was confidence.

"It's a great game," Dom expanded. "Teaches strategy and cooperation. If I ever have a son, I hope he plays. What about you?"

The question was directed at Matt, who was studying the pulp clinging to the side of his glass. "I suppose," he returned. "It's not something I've really thought about."

"Which?" Dom cajoled, grinning. "The son, or having him play?"

"Either." With complete nonchalance, Matt drained his orange juice. "Before you get the son you have other decisions to make...ones that require a lot of long, hard thinking."

Dom chuckled. "Like acquiring a wife?"

"I understand it's a preferable prerequisite."

"So I've heard. What do you think, Eden?"

If it hadn't been for the knot of nerves in her stomach, Eden would have thought the atmosphere quite companionable. The men's tones indicated little more than conversational interest in the subject. Since she wasn't about to put a damper on things by showing any greater concern with it herself, she answered Dom with a teasing smile. "Definitely preferable."

"Yeah," Dom went on. "One of these days I'll stop taking these kinds of assignments and settle down somewhere. Can't raise a family when you're on the move so much."

That's not how Eden sees it, Matt thought, his eyes on her hands as she raised her cup. She had beautiful hands. Soft. Soothing.

"Sure you can," she countered easily. "If that's what you want."

She wanted it all. And, for some reason, Matt didn't doubt that someday she'd have it. In the meantime, though, she was having the strangest effect on the convictions he'd lived with for most of his life. Being fairly conventional in his own thinking, he'd never considered not staying in one place if and when he got married.

The fact that he was sitting there contemplating the subject at all made him uncomfortable. Eden constantly confused him. And he didn't like being confused. It was still a little hard for him to believe he'd walked out on her the way he had the other night. She'd been so willing...

Dom's words snapped Matt back from those disquieting thoughts. "I suppose it'd be possible if you found a woman willing to go along with it," he heard him say. "Can't imagine there are too many around who'd want to pull up roots every couple of years, though. Tell you what..." Leaning forward, he pulled out his wallet, directing his words to the bills he unfolded. "...if I ever meet a woman I want to marry, I'll send her over to talk to you, Eden. Now, if you'll excuse me, I have some things to take care of back at my room."

Eden rose to let Dom slide out. Returning his easy smile along with a quiet "See you in a few minutes," she resettled to finish her coffee. "I like him," she said, unwilling to let silence remind her that everything wasn't quite right between her and Matt.

"Is there anyone you *don't* like?" he teased.

"No," she admitted, relieved to find him receptive. "I don't think there is."

He smiled. Not the knee-weakening smile that turned her insides to jelly, but a rather rueful one that made her think he'd known the answer before she'd given it to him.

Encouraged, she started to expand on the opening he'd given her, only to find her heart pounding in her throat when she saw him reach toward her. A moment later, her heart sank. Her hand was lying by the bills Dom had tossed onto the check. It was the check Matt picked up.

"Come on, kid," he said, holding the left side of his tan corduroy jacket as he stood up so his gun wouldn't be exposed to the restaurant's other customers. "We'd better get going, too. I can't tell you how excited I am about the prospect of spending the day at a shopping mall."

Eden tried, but for the life of her she couldn't respond to his slightly sarcastic comment. Kid. He'd actually called her kid! That made her sound like his little sister.

She shot him a sideways glance, catching nothing in his expression that might reveal his protected thoughts. What had happened between them the other night was clearly a closed issue. But she wasn't at all sure she liked the way he was choosing to handle it. Was he really as unaffected by her presence as he appeared to be?

That question nagged at her for hours—which was the amount of time Niki seemed determined to spend at the enormous mall he'd selected from the local city map. Eden didn't think anyone could out-shop her, but had shopping been an Olympic event, Niki would have taken the gold medal hands down. There were over a hundred stores situated around a sunken arcade and glass atrium, and by three that afternoon, Eden could have sworn they'd hit some of them twice.

Not wanting to attract any undue attention to the little entourage, the men had abandoned their usual three-piece suits. Only Niki, blissfully unconcerned with how solemn he looked with his white scarf draped over the collar of his black overcoat, hadn't completely forsaken formality. As for the rest of them, it was impossible to tell that the six men in jeans and casual jackets were actually Soviet and American security agents. They blended in so well with the crowd of shoppers that, half the time, Eden didn't even know where they were. That's why she was a little startled when she heard Matt's voice behind her. She hadn't even known he'd come into the store with her and Niki and Mr. Androvich.

"How much longer is he going to keep this up?"

Eden turned from the display of men's ties she was perusing, holding up the two she was trying to decide between. Matt was frowning across the aisle to where Niki was trying on dinner jackets.

Thinking Matt looked a bit like her father did when he tired of being towed through stores by her mother, she turned back to the ties. She was in her element. If there was one thing she loved to do, it was hunt for a bargain. This whole rack was on sale. "What's the matter? Your feet hurt?"

"No."

With a knowing smile, she critically eyed her selections. "That's the excuse Dad always gives Mom. I can't decide which one of these to get for him. Which do you like better?"

"That one," he said, pointing to the subtler of the two. Releasing a martyred sigh when he saw the salesman waiting on Niki appear with another armload of clothing, he jammed his hands into his pockets. A moment later, he wandered off, making himself invisible again. He'd only sought her out to ask if there was an end in sight. She already knew he regarded this little expedition as compromising one long, trying day.

It didn't make any sense at all to Eden. She told herself last night that it would be better if Matt left her alone, yet she'd hoped he'd stay with her for a while—maybe help her pick out a shirt to go with the tie. He may have professed a typically male dislike of shopping, but as well-dressed as he usually was, he obviously spent some time in the better clothing stores. The cableknit, sky-blue sweater he wore with his jacket and slightly faded jeans was not only expensive, it also matched his eyes perfectly.

Out of sheer perversity, she put the tie he'd selected back on the rack, taking the one with the bolder stripes to the saleslady, who looked as though she was about to approach Matt with more than a potential sale in mind. Not particularly pleased with the appreciative smile lighting his eyes when the woman stopped in front of him, Eden told herself it was totally unfair of him to start cooperating with her wishes before she could tell him what they were. Not once in the last thirty-six hours had he given her a single chance to exhibit the caution she'd all but forgotten about.

"I'll take this one," she told the woman who was appraising the breadth of Matt's shoulders.

Matt shook his head at her intended purchase, then turned and walked away. From where he stopped several feet away, she could feel him watching her. There was little pleasure to be taken in that, though. He always watched her—just like he always kept an eye on the Russian man who seemed intent on buying a lifetime supply of cummer-bunds.

It was nearly an hour before Niki, having received the proprietor's assurances through her that the alterations to his new tuxedo would be complete by Wednesday, decided it was time to leave the store. Ivan and Boris, each carrying some of Niki's previous acquisitions, followed him and Sergei through the mall. Matt was somewhere behind them, as were Steve and Dom.

Between the January white sales and the inclement weather, Eden could have sworn that half of Philadelphia was squeezed into the covered complex. Two little old ladies held each other up as they resolutely maintained their sedate pace against the crowds. A group of pink- and blue-haired boys bore down on them, parting in the middle as they passed, then regrouped to gawk at a bunch of high-school girls giggling at a lingerie display. Families. Singles. Couples. The place was filled with young people, people who'd forgotten what young was all about, and those of every possible age in between. They scurried or strolled from one place to the next, or rested on the long benches placed strategically throughout the bustling mall.

A little boy of two or three darted in front of her, his bright yellow sweatshirt announcing to the world that he was a Future Fullback. His parents obviously saw a football career in the offing and, because he moved so quickly, Eden thought he might just make it in about seventeen years.

Remembering her conversation with Dom and Matt that morning, she smiled to herself as the child disappeared

among the forest of legs. The little boy looked like a handful, and for no logical reason at all she found herself wondering what Matt had been like as a child. Aggressive, no
doubt. And inquisitive. Just like the little boy who reap-
peared again when she moved forward a few dozen feet.

Eden really didn't want to keep thinking about Matt.
Spotting a poster announcing Niki's concerts, she was preparing to mention it when Niki turned around to wait for
her. But it wasn't Niki or Matt occupying her thoughts now.
It was the child in the yellow sweatshirt. He was standing a
few yards away from her at the top of the escalator, innocently fascinated with the moving stairs. He was far too
young to realize the danger they presented and no one else
even seemed to notice he was there. Not one of the people
composing the near constant stream of downward-bound
passengers paid him the slightest bit of attention.

Eden glanced behind her, fully expecting a harried par-
ent to come chasing after the pint-size bundle of curiosity.
There were plenty of likely looking prospects around, but as
crowded as it was, it was really impossible to tell who the
tow-headed child belonged to. As it was, there was no time
to figure it out. Her glance swung back to the future fullback just as he took a tentative step forward. He made the
first step all right, but an instant later, the forward motion
testing his precarious balance, he landed on his well-padded
bottom. His startled whimper came just as Eden, nearly
knocking Niki over, reached the escalator and scooped him
up, softly assuring him everything was all right.

Everything might have been all right, too—except that,
when Eden grabbed for him, she had to get on the escalator
herself to keep from going over headfirst, and she and the
child were now moving down to the lower level. Three teen-
agers promptly crowded behind her, and more passengers
followed them.

"My baby!"

"That's him!" a gray-haired lady in a mink coat screeched over the first shout. "Oh, Ethel! It's Nikolai Dubikov!"

"My baby! Help somebody! That woman's taking my child!"

"Who's Dubiloff?" one of the kids muttered, craning his neck to see several very large men close ranks around the bearded man at the top of the escalator.

"Please, somebody!"

The sound of his mother's frantic voice frightened the little boy far more than had his minor fall. For a split second he looked at Eden, his bottom lip quivering, and then he let out a screech that threatened to break every piece of glass within fifty yards. The couple in front of Eden turned to glare at her, and just as she started to tell them he'd fallen down while trying to soothe the squalling child, she glanced up to see Niki, Sergei, Ivan and Matt blocking the top of the escalator while a blond woman in a maroon ski jacket shrieked at them to get out of her way.

Panic was a fairly universal language. Niki might not have understood exactly what the woman was saying, but he comprehended her fear. He'd apparently seen what had happened and was trying to explain what had happened, with absolutely no success since he was speaking in Russian. Sergei, who hadn't seen, was trying to assess the situation and translate it to the frantic woman. Matt, grabbing a handful of the woman's parka pulled her onto the steps and started after Eden. "Stop yelling, lady," she heard him order over the tops of the kids' heads. "We'll get her at the bottom."

"*Pourquoi moi?*" Eden groaned to herself, absently stroking the soft hair of the child whose sticky little hands were getting something chocolate all over the front of her beige jacket. Why me?

It took only about ten more seconds to reach the bottom. Getting off, she started to step aside, only to find the man in front of her turning to grab her arm. "You're staying right here," he told her, while his girlfriend or whoever she was tried to pull him back.

"Stay out of it, Larry," the woman said, looking a bit frantic herself. "It's none of our business."

"My baby!" The blond woman with Matt snatched the child from Eden's arms. "How dare you, you awful person! How dare you take my—"

"I didn't...!"

"Take it easy," Matt cut in, impatiently hauling both women out of the flow of traffic.

"I want her arrested! Somebody get the police!"

"I'll do it," Larry the Hero offered.

"Hang on a minute." Matt, still holding Eden's arm, reached into his back pocket. He shot her a look that clearly said, *Keep your mouth shut* and flipped out his wallet to expose his ID and a very impressive-looking badge. "I'll take care of it," he told the man, then turned to the overwrought mother. "Look, lady, there's more than one person at fault here. Where were you?"

Matt had a way of looking at people that made them want to shrink back into the nearest wall. Being the recipient of that accusing glare, the woman lowered her voice by a couple of decibels. Even without the badge he'd flashed at her, Matt's air of unquestionable authority allowed for nothing less than total cooperation. "What do you mean?"

"Why weren't you watching him?"

The woman reddened. "I only turned my back for a minute."

"A minute too long, obviously."

The rebuke had the woman coloring even more, but the coolness in Matt's eyes vanished when he saw the child cuddle closer to his mother. Reaching over to ruffle the little guy's hair, he almost smiled. "They move awfully fast at this age. How old is he?"

"Two and a half," the woman replied, watching Matt with a mixture of respect and fear. "He's . . . he's pretty active."

"My nephew just turned three," he told her while Eden stared in total disbelief. He'd never said a thing about having a nephew, and here he was talking about his family to a total stranger! "My sister says the terrible twos are the worst." His expression hardened again, just enough for the woman to realize that, while he was quite capable of understanding her situation, he still considered her responsible for the unfortunate incident. "You keep a closer eye on him."

"Yes, sir," came the quiet reply. "Thank you."

Clutching her child, the blond backed away. She didn't even glance at Eden, but offered Matt a faltering smile before she turned and disappeared into the gaping crowd. She'd actually looked a little scared of him when he'd admonished her for not keeping track of her son. But the woman had gotten off easy. Eden had the feeling Matt was saving his real irritation for her. If there was one thing she knew he didn't like, it was this kind of confusion.

"I should thank you, too," she offered, wanting to disarm him before he had a chance to explode. If that Larry person had dragged one of the mall guards into this they'd be in the middle of an even bigger mess right now.

"Anytime," he returned, sounding for all the world as if he'd done nothing but pick up something she'd dropped. "We'd better get back upstairs. Think Dubikov's ready to go yet?"

Eden looked at him in total astonishment. Wasn't he even going to yell at her or tell her she was damn lucky he'd been around to straighten out this latest fiasco she'd gotten herself involved in? Wasn't he even going to demand an explanation as to how all of this had come about?

"Did you see what happened?" she asked, thinking he must have.

Taking her arm to lead her to the escalator, he gave her an oblique glance. "No. But, I know you're no more capable of kidnapping a child than I am. From what Sergei was trying to say for Niki, it sounded like the kid fell and you picked him up. When I heard the mother and saw you, it was pretty obvious what had happened."

"It wasn't so obvious to her."

"I know," he agreed, far too easily as far as Eden was concerned. "And as upset as she was, it would have taken too long to wait for her to calm down and listen to explanations."

"Then you're not mad at me?"

"Should I be?"

"No," she answered, surprised to hear the uncertainty in her voice. "But don't you think you were a little hard on her?"

"Considering that she was too involved in her conversation to notice her son was missing, I don't think so. When I saw her a few minutes ago, she wasn't paying attention to anything except whatever it was her friend was laughing about." They stepped onto the escalator together, Matt keeping his eyes straight ahead while Eden frowned at him.

Matt had a remarkable memory. He could scan a crowd and remember every single face he'd seen. But he seemed to have noticed a lot more than usual about the woman who was only one of hundreds of others. "You were watching her?"

"More or less." He smiled ever so slightly, as if he were entertaining some privately amusing thought. "She did a pretty fair job of filling out those jeans."

Since he didn't so much as glance at her, Eden's effort to keep her expression as bland as his was wasted. "I didn't notice," was all she said, irritated that he had. Matt was free to look at whomever and whatever he chose. And if he chose to look at some irresponsible mother's backside, that was his business. It just didn't sit very well with Eden to realize that the woman had gotten more of a reaction out of Matt than she had.

Telling herself she should be grateful that Matt hadn't decided to unleash his considerable wrath on her again, Eden went about the rest of the day trying to force an enthusiasm she simply didn't feel. For all practical purposes, Matt was acting almost... brotherly.

Niki's attitude toward her seemed to be developing along those same lines. With him, though, she enjoyed it. He was also becoming more dependent on her. No matter where they went or what they did for the next three days, he was always at her side, relying on her company and her smile to ease the pains of living in a fishbowl. Eden didn't know how he could stand his almost total lack of privacy, and when she commented on that to Matt, he admitted that he'd never be able to survive that way, but said it was the price Niki seemed willing to pay for the opportunity to share his music.

Matt seemed to regard Niki with a fair amount of compassion, something she didn't quite understand, because Niki wasn't the type who invited sympathy. Maybe it was because Matt wasn't the type to be bound down by anything or anyone and he felt a certain inequity with Niki's lack of personal freedom.

"I can't imagine committing myself to something to the point of giving up control over my life," he said with a dismissive chuckle. "I'm surprised he doesn't have claustrophobia."

By Thursday, Eden wasn't so sure Niki was entirely free of that particular disorder. That was why, when the chance for a moment's escape presented itself, she didn't even question his need to take it.

The orchestra was taking its first break of the afternoon. They'd spent two hours going over the same movement, and the break was more than deserved. Niki was a perfectionist, but today even perfection hadn't been good enough. Now, seeing him motion to her from the wings, she left the stage to join him. As soon as she reached his side, he gave her a strangely agitated smile and, glancing around to make sure no one was listening, lowered his voice to a whisper. "You will come with me for a few moments?"

Eden fully expected to see one of the Surveillance Six materialize through the heavy black drapes. Incredible as it was, Sergei, Ivan and Boris were nowhere to be seen. Neither were Matt, Steve and Dom. Apparently they'd all hit the coffee machine at once. That's where Matt had told her he was going when he'd sauntered off a minute ago.

Assuming Niki simply wanted to get some fresh air without having a mini-army breathing down his neck, she let him lead her through the side exit, and out into the chill, winter air. Even prisoners got time off for good behavior and it wasn't like he'd be wandering the streets alone. She was with him.

A second doorway, this one recessed and covered by the extended roof, was off to their right. Niki hurried them toward it while Eden, beginning to wonder if he had something other than a quick, unescorted walk in mind, belatedly thought that this might not be a very good idea after all.

"Maybe we should go back," she suggested when they reached the small shelter.

"Not yet." He turned to her, and she was so startled by what she saw in his eyes that she promptly forgot about possible consequences.

There was no time to analyze why it was there, but his fear and desperation were very real. They were every bit as apparent as the plea in his voice.

"I must ask something of our friendship, Eden. You are truly my friend, are you not?"

She could only nod, wanting to assure this huge man with the frightened eyes that she was. He asked if he could trust her and again, puzzled, she nodded. Then his words came so rapidly she could barely translate them to herself fast enough to keep up with him.

"I have an older brother, Pasha," he told her. "He left Russia thirty years ago. Before he left, he made me promise that no matter what happened, I would practice my violin. 'You play if they take away everything. You play if they send our family to Siberia because of what I must do. If they take your violin, you play in your head. Someday, the world will know your music.' That is what he said to me. I loved my brother and because he was older and knew more than I, I listened."

A hundred questions hung on Eden's lips. Asking the first one that came to mind, she put the rest on hold. "Did anything happen to your family after your brother defected?"

"There is no time to explain that now." Assuring her that the situation could have been much worse than it was, he hurried on. "Pasha was what you call a dreamer. He never showed much ambition, so his leaving was of little importance to anyone except my family. Because he is still important to us . . . and to me," he continued solemnly, "because I owe him so much, I need you to find him. Not so I can see him. Androvich will never allow it. But for you to give him news of us, to tell him all is well and we've never forgotten him.''

There was clearly no one else he could turn to, and it didn't even occur to Eden to refuse Niki's request. In the two minutes it took him to explain about Pasha, she went from sympathy to disbelief to indignation. Not only was she angry over the way a proud man like Niki had been forced to beg for help, but it offended her sense of justice to think that something as impersonal as politics should keep two brothers apart.

''I'll do everything I can,'' she promised, strengthening that assurance with a smile that probably looked more confident than she felt.

''You will tell no one?''

''Of course not.'' She wouldn't dream of jeopardizing Niki that way.

The moment Niki had her agreement, he was talking again, too agitated to show much relief. His eyes kept darting to the outside stage door; his voice was furtive.

He had no idea where his brother was living, except that he thought he might be somewhere on the West Coast because he'd once mentioned California. Eden didn't have a clue as to how she'd find Pasha. Before she could spend any time thinking about that, though, she and Niki had to get back inside before someone discovered they were missing.

That thought came about thirty seconds too late.

She heard the exit door crash open. Then came the furious beat of footsteps pounding on the sidewalk and an instant after they stepped out of the doorway, she and Niki were surrounded by six stony-faced men who appeared perfectly capable of creating all sorts of bodily mayhem.

Eden had been in hot water before, but from the look of things she was in enough now to cover Mount Everest. Niki apparently realized that, too, but he was much quicker to cover the guilt in his expression than Eden was.

The first demand came from Androvich. Whether Matt was learning Russian or he'd just lucked out on the translation didn't much matter. He got Androvich's "What in the hell is going on here?" word perfect.

Niki gave Eden a theatrical smile, his eyes beseeching her to go along with what he was about to do. Touching her cheek and letting his hand fall melodramatically, he turned to offer his explanation to the little man with the furious gray eyes.

It wasn't those gray eyes that Eden found so frightening. It was the blue ones that held absolutely no trace of emotion as they bore down on her. She'd expected to see exasperation or reproach or displeasure, but the absence of any discernible responses made Matt's expression as cold as the Alps in winter. The frost in his voice when he quietly ordered her to tell him what Niki had said didn't do much for her already questionable composure, either.

Trying to translate Niki's words wasn't easy. Not with half a dozen Soviet and American security agents looking at you as if you'd just sold out to the other side. It was intimidating to say the least, but very enlightening, too. Like the proverbial bolt out of the blue the reason why everyone was keeping such a close eye on Niki hit her. They must all know about his brother and, when they hadn't been able to find Niki inside, had thought he'd tried to defect, too. It was no wonder they all seemed so upset.

"Eden," Matt repeated when she didn't comply with his request for a translation.

"He said," Androvich offered, his coolness slowly thawing from his formidable glare, "it is a pity a man cannot be alone with a beautiful woman. He is sorry for the problem, but who can blame him? He is only a man."

He is also a hell of a ham, Eden thought, treating herself to a little relief when she saw how easily Sergei had fallen for the line. Niki's reputation with women was no secret and Androvich seemed to relax with the realization that this had been nothing more than a short, clandestine meeting and not an attempt to escape.

"We will go back inside now," Androvich told her, disapproval heavily evident in his tone. "And we will not repeat incident again. It is nothing to do with you, Eden Michaels. I find your company pleasant, as does Nikolai. He cannot take time from his practice, though. Unfortunate, but this is the way it must be."

"I understand," she told him, far too nervous to smile at the absurd warning. He was telling her, as diplomatically as possible, that an affair with Niki was out of the question.

With a terse "Good," he motioned Niki ahead of him, leaving her vulnerable to the glare that had yet to leave Matt's eyes.

The harshness in his voice complemented that daunting expression perfectly. "What were you doing out here?"

"I thought it was obvious," she answered, focusing on his tie tack.

"Try again, Eden."

Androvich may have bought Niki's act, but Matt hadn't. She wasn't acting at all like a woman who'd just been torn from the arms of a potential lover. Oh, she looked guilty all right. But her eyes didn't have that dark longing he'd seen when he'd held her—and she hadn't responded at all when Niki touched her cheek. Every time Matt had done that, she'd unconsciously turned her head toward the caress. "What were you doing out here?" he repeated.

"Matt," she began patiently, hugging her arms together to ward off the chill. "I'm not going to talk about this. It's freezing out here and if you want to stand around and catch pneumonia that's fine with me. I'm going inside."

"Eden," he growled, chasing her, "answer me."

"Oh, all right." Pulling open the door, she heard the string section tuning up again. In another minute or two, she'd be busy with the conductor and Matt would have to leave her alone.

"Well?" he prodded, sounding a little less angry now that he thought she was about to cooperate. "What were you doing?"

"Giving away state secrets."

Eden knew from the way Matt was glaring holes in her back that he wasn't going to accept that flip little comment. She also knew that sometime between now and whenever he decided to confront her again, she'd have to come up with some plausible explanation for why she and Niki had gone outside like that. For three days, she'd been hoping Matt would try to get her alone. Now that she was sure he would, the prospect lost a considerable amount of its appeal.

Seven

Eden had been in her hotel room for a full five minutes before she heard the expected knock at her door. She wasn't
at all surprised when Matt didn't wait for her to invite him
in after she opened it. But his tone caught her off guard. He
sounded like he looked—a little too calm.

"All right, Eden." With deceptive casualness, he walked
right past her. Then, crossing his arms, he leaned against the
long, mirrored dresser opposite the king-size bed. "What
were you and Dubikov doing?"

In the two hours since she and Niki had been caught outside the rehearsal hall, Eden had conjured up and abandoned an amazing variety of harebrained excuses in
preparation for that question. Never having been able to
fabricate with any credibility, she'd finally concluded that
the best way to handle this was to act as if the incident was
completely insignificant. Even if she hadn't given Niki her
word that she wouldn't tell anyone about what he'd asked

of her, she certainly couldn't tell Matt. The first thing he'd do was tell her to forget it.

Unwilling to lie, she chose to evade. "Talking," she returned, acting as nonchalant as possible by picking up her jacket from the beige and blue patterned bedspread and heading for the closet.

"About what?"

A piece of lint clung to the lapel. Removing it, she put the jacket on a hanger, smoothed the collar and hung it on the rod. "Music," she replied, because it had come up. "Oh, there they are!" A half-eaten package of peanuts was pulled from the pocket, along with the scarf she'd worn earlier. "I was wondering where I'd put these."

From the corner of her eye, she saw Matt take a deep breath. He was no more interested in the bag of peanuts than he was in letting her change the subject. "Eden," he began with forced patience, "you and Dubikov talk about music all the time. I find it a little hard to believe that he had to ditch his guard to discuss it a while ago."

"Maybe he wanted some air."

"If that's all he wanted, why'd you look so guilty when we found you?"

"I think you're confusing guilt with surprise. If anything, I was just startled when you guys all started running toward us." That was certainly honest enough. Having all those big men converge on her and Niki the way they did *had* been rather alarming.

In three long strides Matt was beside her, taking the scarf she was trying to fold and dropping it onto the bed. Hands on her shoulders, he turned her to face him. He didn't look angry, and that worried her a little. She could deal with him when he was irritated; it was his skillful authority she didn't quite know how to handle.

"I know you," he announced flatly, "and I don't buy what you're saying now any more than I bought that cock-and-bull story Androvich fell for. The idea of you and Dubikov sneaking out for a lover's tryst is about as plausible as me filling in for him at a concert."

It was clear enough that he recognized the platonic nature of her relationship with Niki. But Matt's words, combined with his touch, finally succeeded in raising her defenses. His grip on her shoulders was totally impersonal, nothing more than a way of holding her in place. "Maybe you should believe what Niki said," she snapped. Eden knew Niki saw her as only a friend, but just because Matt didn't want her didn't mean another man might not find her desirable. "It's not exactly impossible he might be interested in more than my mind, you know."

She tried to turn away. Matt wouldn't let her. He also wouldn't let himself lose his temper, though she was certainly testing it now. He had little enough control when it came to Eden without her deliberately pushing him like this. "Are you saying he wants you in his bed?"

Leave it to Matt to narrow something down like that. Nothing was ever gray to him. Only black or white. "No," she had to admit, and twisting her shoulders, stepped out of his grip. Snatching back the scarf, she muttered, in French, *"But I wish you did."*

Giving the fabric a snap, she'd just started to fold it when she heard Matt return, in French, *"What makes you think I don't?"*

Three things hit Eden all at once: a touch of chagrin at her bold announcement; surprise that Matt had quite obviously understood it; and a very strong suspicion that she'd misinterpreted his question. Slowly pulling her glance from the length of green patterned silk in her hands, she turned her head toward him. His expression told her nothing. "What did you say?"

"You heard me." Sounding every bit as defensive as he looked, he jammed his hands into his pockets. The motion was followed by the dull clink of change being shuffled around. "But that has absolutely nothing to do with what we're talking about now. You've got a way of getting yourself into messes, Eden. But this one's got the potential for being an all-out disaster."

If he wanted her, then why wasn't he doing anything about it? "How do you know that?" she challenged, thinking there was no way she'd get an answer to her silent question at the moment. "You don't even know what he wants."

"Don't I? Hasn't it occurred to you that there's a reason we've been watching him so closely?"

"It didn't occur to me until a while ago," she muttered, more concerned with what was going on between them than with the matter to which he was so obviously referring. Beneath the demands and evasions lay a basic difference in their attitudes. "You know, Matt, I've never seen much point in assuming something bad will happen until a situation demands that kind of thinking. But you seem to assume the worst, then let the matter prove itself otherwise. Can't you . . . ?"

"I can't afford to wait until after the fact," he cut in. "It's too damn risky. Did he ask you to help him?"

"What he asked me for," she advised, feeding off of Matt's growing agitation, "was my word. And since I gave it to him, I'm not about to break it. Unlike some other people I know, he trusts me."

At her last words, Matt's jaw tensed. That unquestioning trust of hers was going to land her in a whole heap of trouble one of these days. "You didn't answer me," he reminded tersely.

"I didn't think it was necessary. You seem to have everything all figured out."

"Did you tell him you would?"

"Would what?"

"Help him," he shot back, exasperated.

"Yes!" she returned, more sharply than she'd intended. "There's no reason not to. It's not going to hurt anybody."

Matt stared at her in utter disbelief. "Not hurt anybody?" he repeated, his voice rising before he could stop it. "How do you figure that contributing to the disintegration of a political relationship isn't going to hurt anybody? This isn't like getting caught with a bunch of flowers or having some idiot woman think you're kidnapping her kid. If you try to help him defect, you'll have the Soviet Consulate and..."

"That's not what he wants!"

"...the whole State Department down on your...what?"

"He doesn't want to defect! There's no way he'd ever do that." Insisting to herself that getting upset wouldn't help anything, she deliberately lowered her voice. "I told you that what he wants is perfectly harmless. It's not going to jeopardize him or me or anyone or anything else. Can't you just accept that? Can't you believe me?"

She didn't know if it was her questions or her assurance that Niki wasn't going to bolt that took the wind out of Matt's sails. Slowly pulling his hands from his pockets, he pushed one through his hair as he carefully considered her.

She was telling the truth. He'd have staked his life on that. He knew she couldn't lie to him. He doubted she could lie to anyone. But it was her voice, the plea he'd heard in it only a moment ago, that cut through his irritation. She asked him to believe her. And belief took trust.

"I want to," he heard himself say before he could think better of it.

"Then do," she urged, her tone gently accusing. "Take some of that pressure off yourself and have a little faith in someone else for a change. You can tighten your own reins, but you can't control everyone else's."

"Is that what you think I do?"

The question surprised her. So did the stricken look in his eyes.

"I shouldn't have said that," she apologized, and started to turn away. The feel of Matt's hand sliding up her arm stopped her.

"Is that what you think I do?" he repeated, curving his fingers over her shoulder. "Try to control people?"

She shook her head, her heart beating a little erratically at his nearness. "No, I...I meant the demands you place on yourself by not..."

Tipping her chin toward him when she hesitated, he quietly asked, "Not what?"

"Accepting," she said simply.

He raised his hand, leaving it suspended only inches from her jaw. "That's asking a lot, Eden." The back of his knuckles grazed her cheek, and her head turned almost imperceptibly into the caress. Enormously satisfied with that telling response, he allowed himself to touch the delicate line of her jaw. "If I just blindly accept, then I..."

"Lose control," she completed for him.

Her skin felt like satin, her hair like strands of silk when he pushed his fingers upward over the back of her neck. Oddly enough, he didn't feel threatened by her insight this time. In a way, it was almost a relief to have her realize how tenaciously he clung to what he'd fought so hard to attain. If a man didn't have authority over himself, he became vulnerable.

"Control is something I seem to have precious little of lately." He drew a long, slow breath. With it came that clean, flowery scent she wore, that essence of spring and light and warmth. "Why do you suppose that is?"

Matt didn't like it when he couldn't comprehend something. Eden knew that. Just as she knew by the way his darkening eyes shifted over her face that it was entirely possible she was the reason for his confusion.

Smiling softly at the grim line of his mouth, she laid her hand on his chest. "Don't worry about it. You don't have to understand everything, you know."

"Believe me," he whispered, sliding his arm around her back. "I don't. But I sure as hell plan on figuring it out."

His words faded, along with a fair amount of his restraint when his hand slipped down to the curve of her bottom. Drawing her sharply against him, he pulled her upward, his other hand delving into her hair as he lowered his head. In the next breath, his mouth was on hers.

Sweet. She tasted soft and sweet and so willing that Matt couldn't begin to tell himself he shouldn't be doing this. But he was only human and he couldn't deny the swift stab of desire coursing through him when her tongue darted out to meet his.

Whatever it was Eden was up to with Niki had become the farthest thing from Matt's mind. What he didn't understand now was how he'd ever managed to keep himself away from her for so long. To touch her, to hold her was all he really wanted to do. No, he thought, fitting her slender body to the hardened contours of his own, he wanted more than that. He wanted her naked and lying beneath him. He wanted to possess her, to lose himself in her softness. Maybe once he'd satisfied his physical need, he wouldn't be so obsessed with everything about her.

"God, woman," he breathed, taking little sips from the corner of her mouth. She tilted her head, inviting his exploration of her throat. "The things you do to me."

"I'm not doing anything," he heard her whisper, her arms curving around his neck.

"You'd have a hard time convincing my body of that."

He thrust forward, his need boldly announcing itself against her. Keeping his palm pressed to the base of her spine, he felt her shudder.

"Matt . . ."

He captured his name with his mouth, refusing to let her say anything that might refute the message her body was relaying to him. Within seconds he discovered that whatever she'd intended to say was only meant as encouragement. She returned his kiss fully, allowing his tongue to tantalize and seek.

When he finally lifted his head, his breath on her cheek felt as shallow as her own. He framed her face with his hands and pulled back a little more. Eden looked up at him, her eyes glittering green and heavy with the desire she couldn't hide. I wonder, she thought, if I could ever hide anything from him.

"I'm going to make love with you, Eden."

She leaned into him, relishing the feel of his lips feverishly tracing her temple, her ear. So gentle. "I know," she sighed, feeling the heat of his hand as it covered her breast. She liked the way he said that. With. Not to. Together. Shared. "I know."

His hand moved between them, his fingers working at the buttons of her blouse. She knew she was shaking. Every breath she drew attested to that. And when she pulled back a little so he could free the clasp of her bra, she discovered that he was trembling, too.

The clasp finally gave, his movements measured as he slowly edged the fabric aside. Hunger. Stark and raw, it was carved in his beautiful, tensed features as he let his eyes drift over her. But more than that, there was need. It was in his touch—and in his kiss, when he pulled her back to him, crushing her mouth to his.

I love him. She didn't know how it had happened, or even when. But sometime during the past two weeks, somewhere between Boston and Philadelphia, she'd fallen in love with him. Hopelessly. Irrevocably. Completely.

She should have been startled by that realization. Instead, she simply let the feeling sink in, absorbing it while shirts and skirt and slacks were slowly stripped away to allow the deliciously slow explorations that accompanied each discarded piece of fabric. She had no idea how long it took before the last few scraps of material were discarded. She was aware only of Matt and how weak her legs felt when his lips followed the wisp of nylon past her hips. She felt herself reaching out to him, her only means of support his arms when he lifted her onto the bed and flipped back the covers.

The sheets felt cool, his body warm as he stretched out beside her, burning along her side while he continued the maddening stroke of his hand over her thigh.

"You're so soft," he said, wonder threading through the huskiness of his voice. "So incredibly soft."

"Please, Matt," she begged, feeling the heat escalate when his fingers slipped between her legs.

"Soon, honey," he promised, boldly ignoring her plea. "We're going to take this slow. I've wanted you for too long." He traced a path of searing kisses from her throat to the soft skin between her breasts. With agonizing deliberation, he pulled one turgid peak into his mouth, flicking his tongue around it, then drawing in and releasing it again.

"Soon," he repeated, coiling his leg around hers while his lips continued their tantalizing play.

Wrapped in a hazy cocoon of sensation, she could only cling to him. Beneath her hands she could feel the tense muscles in his shoulders. That tension seemed to fill his entire body, each stroke of her hand increasing it until it felt as if the formidable control he exerted over himself would snap at any second. Needing him to share that control with her, she let her fingers drift around his side, flattening against his hard stomach. But the instant they started moving lower, he grabbed her hand, pulling it up to pin it beside her head.

A slightly wicked smile touched his mouth. "It'll be over in two seconds if you do that."

"Then later," she promised and heard the groan come from deep within his chest when he slipped his hand under her hips.

He felt her lift to him and, within seconds, he was inside her, his intention to take it slowly completely shattered by her husky words. There was no time for thought, only feeling. It spiraled through him, built with a speed that hurled him toward a place where consciousness didn't exist, then exploded in a white hot sensation of heat and light. Eden was there with him. He'd carried her to that place and she clung to him, his name on her lips as they began the long, slow descent to reality.

But the reality Matt returned to wasn't quite the same as it had always been before. He didn't feel the vague disassociation that had always followed physical culmination—that need to keep himself separate. Stroking her hair and gently kissing her, he also discovered that he didn't want to offer the practiced platitudes that usually prefaced his retreat. They weren't right for Eden. "You okay?" he whispered and, propping himself up on his elbows, saw a languid smile touch her lips.

"Better than okay," she returned, wondering if there was a word to describe how she felt. Beneath the contentment, the wonder of feeling so absolutely complete, though, ran a tiny thread of wariness. "Why the frown?"

"Because I just thought of something that . . . uh . . ." He hesitated, his glance darting away from her as he tried to find a delicate way to put his question. He couldn't believe he hadn't thought of it earlier. "I know it's a little late to be asking, but do I have anything to worry about?"

She knew what he was referring to, and under the circumstances he had every right to ask. The last thing she wanted was an unscheduled pregnancy, but for some reason she couldn't begin to fathom, it hurt a little to see the flicker of panic he hadn't been able to hide. She knew Matt would never shirk a responsibility, but that wasn't the kind of commitment she wanted from him. "You have nothing to worry about," she assured him, feeling the muscles in his back relax.

Acknowledging his relief by brushing his lips across her forehead, he pushed his arm under her, rolling them both onto their sides. The sheets rustled as he pulled them up to cover them, and realizing that he wasn't getting up, Eden breathed a relieved sigh of her own.

"So," he began, nudging her head to his shoulder, "you're not going to tell me what you and Niki are up to, huh?"

He was smiling. She could hear it in his voice. But what struck her—other than the fact that they were more or less discussing business in bed—was that this was the first time Matt hadn't referred to Niki as "Dubikov." "Unh-uh," she mumbled, the slight shake of her head causing the hair on his chest to tickle her cheek. "I can't." Then, wanting to get him off that topic, she glanced up at the dark stubble shadowing his jaw. "Why didn't you tell me you speak French?"

"You never asked," he pointed out reasonably and, guiding her head back down, ignored her attempt to switch subjects. "I'm just supposed to take your word for it that it's nothing I need to be concerned about?"

Resigned, she murmured, "Is that so impossible?"

"I guess not." Drawing his fingers down her arm, he lazily added, "Especially since I don't seem to have any choice."

Eden knew how much that bothered him. "Tell you what. If it looks like it's going to cause even the slightest problem, I promise to tell Niki I can't help him and that will be the end of it." The solid muscles of his stomach twitched as she feathered her fingers over his abdomen. With no small amount of satisfaction, she realized that her touch affected him, too. "I never break a promise."

I don't, either, he thought, tensing even more when she tentatively edged her hand downward. She nuzzled closer, the tip of her tongue grazing his flat, male nipple. That's why I don't want to make any I might not be able to keep.

Turning her roughly in his arms, he tasted the smile on her lips. For the first time in his life, he found himself struggling between what he wanted and what he might need.

"Oh, Barbara," Eden groaned into the phone. With her free hand curved around the high, halter-style collar of her backless, green velvet evening gown, she glanced over her bare shoulder to make sure no one had entered the marble-tiled vestibule where she was standing. The pay phone in the posh and crowded restaurant was one of those open things just outside the rest rooms and not particularly conducive to private conversations. "You can't find *any* information about him?"

Dead-ends. Eden had run into more of them than the
maze she'd worked in Sunday's paper. In the last five days,
she'd called directory assistance in every major city on the
West Coast and more obscure towns, communities and
burgs than she could count. Barbara was her last hope.

"Sorry," her friend returned, apology heavy in her low
voice. "I went through everything we have here, but all I
found was a copy of an old newspaper clipping somebody
had given Harry. All it said was that Pasha Dubikov sought
political asylum after jumping a fishing boat. My code
doesn't access security's files, so I couldn't get a thing out
of the computer. You know, Eden," Barb continued in a
secretive tone, "when I said to call me if you needed anything, I never dreamed you'd want something like this."

"Neither did I. What am I going to do?"

"You could start by telling me exactly what you're up to.
I know," she cut in when she heard Eden's sigh. "You said
you can't, but I'd sure feel better about this if you could."
Having given vent to those reservations, she immediately
dropped them. "In the meantime, to answer your question, I don't know what you can do. You're probably right
in assuming that he's changed his name. If he hadn't, we
could be sure some over-zealous reporter would've figured
out the connection by now and hit the wires with the story.
It'd be a perfect tie-in to the tour."

"Just the kind of publicity the Soviets would love to see,"
Eden drawled.

"Just the kind of thing the department doesn't want,"
Barbara emphasized. "If the higher-ups weren't so concerned about possible negative political repercussions,
they'd have told us more about Pasha. As it is, I didn't even
know about him until you called a few days ago and I
started snooping around Harry's office."

Oh, *Dieu*, Eden moaned to herself. Barbara could have gotten caught doing that! "Don't do anything that'll get you in trouble!"

Barb laughed lightly. "To borrow your line, don't worry about it. A good secretary always knows more than her boss thinks she does. I just wish I could have found something that would do you some good."

"Me, too," Eden sighed, her eyes widening when she saw Matt come around the corner. Raising his eyebrow as he pointed to his watch, he stopped in front of the cigarette machine—a full eighteen inches away from her. "Everything's still on schedule," she went on, her tone now briskly efficient. "Mr. Dubikov is just finishing dinner with the president of the Fine Arts Association. We'll be leaving for the reception in a few minutes."

"Somebody just show up?"

"Yes."

"Matt?"

"Uh-huh."

"How are things going with him?"

"Just fine."

"Just fine?" Barbara echoed, knowing full well that Eden couldn't go into details when the subject they were discussing was standing right beside her. "That doesn't sound too promising."

"Terrific," Eden elaborated, swallowing hard when Matt's hand settled on her waist and his lips touched the back of her neck. It was all she could do to remember what she was going to say when he started nibbling on the lobe of her ear. "I'll call you when we get to Houston tomorrow."

A moment's pause preceded a quiet "Okay. Oh, Eden," Barb added as if she'd just thought of something, "you be careful."

"I will," she returned, frowning a little. Was the warning about Niki? she wondered. Or Matt. "'Bye."

"How are things in Washington?" Matt asked against the side of her neck. His hand wandered over her bare back before sneaking around to her stomach to pull her closer. "I like this dress."

Matt was obviously aware that she'd been checking in with Barb, something he knew she did at least once a day to keep Harry's ulcer from flaring up. But he didn't seem terribly interested in her slightly breathless, "Fine," in response to his first inquiry, or her equally feeble, "Thanks," to his second. He also didn't seem very concerned that someone could come around the corner at any moment. "I can't believe you're doing that," she said, her effort to pull away thwarted by her desire to stay right where she was.

"I've done it before," he pointed out, his warm breath sending alarming little shivers down her neck. "I like your ears." Nuzzling the hair back from the object of his attention, he closed his teeth around the emerald stud, tugging it gently. "A lot."

"That's not what I meant." When he released her earring and looked down at her innocently she gave him a playful shove. "What would you do if Dom or Steve happened to show up?"

"Nothing." With a shrug, he reluctantly stepped aside to let her precede him. Leaving his hand on the small of her back, he nudged her forward. "They've probably figured out what's going on by now. I don't imagine they think I've been sleeping in the hall."

She was certain they didn't. Matt didn't have the luxury of being able to disappear for a few hours without his men knowing where he could be reached. He always returned to his room well before dawn, but it was a dead certainty that neither Dom nor Steve was blind to the changes in Matt's relationship with her.

As he escorted her back into the elegant dining room, leaving her when he joined Dom at their post just inside the dimly lit bar, she felt hope coiling around the other emotions filling her heart. Before now, she hadn't really realized how much Matt had relaxed his guard—how far he'd come since that night somewhere between New York and Boston when he'd felt he had to conceal his attraction for her from everyone else. But instead of letting that hope feed her usual optimism, she found it tempered by a nagging sense of uncertainty. Matt had opened up a lot, but he still held so much of himself inside. It was as if he felt compelled to protect himself somehow, to hold back the part of him that might make him vulnerable to a situation he couldn't control. That was the part she'd yet to reach. The part that, in their most intimate moments, she feared she might never reach.

"Ah, Miss Michaels," stodgy old Mr. Ainsley said at her approach. "I trust you found the telephone?"

"I did," she returned with a distracted smile. "Thank you."

Niki rose, turning slightly as he held her chair so that his back was to Androvich. Lost in her thoughts, it took a moment for the silent inquiry in his eyes to register. When it did, she gave him an almost imperceptible shake of her head and took her seat. The men at the table continued sipping their brandy, not one of them having seen the silent signal that had passed between her and Niki. They didn't even seem to notice the slightly defeated fall of his shoulders, or the sudden determination in Eden's expression when she glanced from Niki to Matt some thirty feet away.

Matt watched her turn toward him as he finished his glass of tonic like the one Dom had ordered. They couldn't have liquor when they were on duty, but the watery concoction helped to give him and Dom the appearance of a patron waiting for a table to open up. Ice cubes clinking as he slowly lowered the glass, he refused to look away until her attention was drawn back to the men at her table. She'd only looked at him for a few seconds, but Matt had held his breath for every one of them.

Dom, sitting across from him, frowned when he saw all expression drain from Matt's face. "Something the matter?"

With a dismissing shake of his head, Matt scowled at the back of his hand. He was surprised to see that it was so steady. "I was just thinking."

"She's really gotten to you, hasn't she?"

There had been a time when Matt would either have ignored that kind of remark, or told the observer that he didn't know what he was talking about. Now, he simply muttered, "Yeah," and tried to dismiss the thought that had scrambled his senses only moments ago.

"What are you going to do about it?"

"I don't know."

"It's a rough one, Matt." Dom's mouth pinched. "We go into this line of work because it sounds interesting, adventurous maybe. But the adventure wears off in a hurry and somewhere between assignments we realize we've been so many places that we can't even remember where home is anymore. And the uncertainty," he went on, his chuckle sounding oddly shallow. "When was the last time you went anywhere without looking over your shoulder? We're on guard so much that it becomes a way of life. It's almost as if we internalize it somehow. I don't know if I honestly remember anymore, but I don't think it's like that on the outside. Eden," he concluded, "is the outside."

I couldn't have put it better myself, Matt thought, smiling wryly at his empty glass. Dom, he'd discovered, had a remarkable talent for finding a person's weakest point. It was a commendable talent for an agent, but a rather disconcerting one for a friend. "I can't tell if you're trying to talk me into, or out of, something, Velasquez."

"Neither. When it comes to women, I try to keep everything superficial. It's easier."

"Isn't that the truth?" Matt muttered.

"You ever been serious before?"

Matt shook his head, realizing after he'd done it that he hadn't thought to question Dom's phrasing. Instead of correcting the assumption that he was serious now, he simply let it pass. "Never met anyone I really wanted to get to know. Even if I had, it wouldn't have been long before it came time to pack up and leave."

"Oh, the side benefits of travel," Dom expanded ironically. Noticing that everyone at Eden's table was getting ready to leave, he pushed his glass aside. "Speaking of which, it looks like this show is about to hit the road again. You get the check and I'll get the cars."

Rising, Dom clapped his hand on Matt's upper arm, letting him know by that typically male gesture that, should he need it, his ear was available. Before Matt met Eden, he'd rarely found it necessary to commiserate with another man when it came to females. And though he and Dom usually found other things to talk about, it was kind of reassuring to have access to an understanding male's opinion.

"Thanks, buddy," Matt mumbled just before Dom walked off, then he waited for Eden and the others to put on their coats while Mr. Ainsley of the Philadelphia Fine Arts Association settled their bill.

Matt wasn't paying much attention to any of that, though. He was too busy telling himself he should be denying what he'd realized the instant he'd caught Eden's eye, instead of standing there quietly accepting it. What he found almost as odd as that failure was that the flash of comprehension had dawned in a crowded restaurant while he and Eden were both working—not while he'd been under the influence of mounting physical desire when she could render him nearly mindless. He was quite lucid right now, every bit as rational as he'd ever been. Yet, he still couldn't deny that what he felt for her went far beyond simple physical desire. It was almost as if she was becoming a part...

"Hey, thanks," a decidedly pleased feminine voice said from behind him. "I don't usually get anything but advice from the ones who don't drink the hard stuff."

Glancing behind him, he saw the cocktail waitress who'd been waiting on him and Dom hold up the generous tip he'd left her. "Advice doesn't pay the rent," he told her, and with a lazy smile turned back to his own thoughts as he followed the woman prompting them out the beveled glass doors.

Matt had never allowed himself to truly care about a woman before. But he knew without a doubt that he did care about Eden and the difference she'd made in his life. There had been times when he felt as if he'd been born thirty-five. Yet, in the past two weeks, he hadn't felt a single trace of that weariness.

Wariness, however, was something he'd felt a lot of lately and that discomforting feeling increased every time he saw the silent signals that passed between Eden and Niki. Remembering the one they'd shared a few minutes ago, he had the awful feeling that whatever it was they were up to wasn't going very well.

The problem, as far as Eden was concerned, was that it wasn't "going" at all. "Matt," she began, the gentle pressure of her hand on his arm drawing him to a halt as soon

as they stepped outside. Waiting until everyone else was at
the limos parked at the curb, she quickly stepped in front of
him, keeping him under the fringed blue awning. "I need
you to occupy Mr. Androvich for me for a minute or two.
Please," she pleaded, seeing the skepticism swiftly shadowing his features.

Matt had been absolutely wonderful about not pressing
her to tell him what Niki wanted. Oh, she was sure he'd been
tempted, but not once had he given in to the curiosity that
would have driven her nuts by now. He was, however, fully
within his rights to pose a tense inquiry at this particular request.

"Why?"

"Matt," she cajoled in a singsong way that somehow
added two inflections to the single vowel in his name. "Just
do it. Please?"

"What are you going to do?"

"I'll explain later. Just get him away from Niki and me at
the reception. Tell him you're confirming our departure
time in the morning. Or... Oh, I don't know. You can think
of something. Aren't you guys supposed to be good at de-
ception?"

He completely ignored her question. "I'll do it on one
condition." Nodding when Steve motioned for them to
hurry up, he let his hand run the length of her coat sleeve.
"That you don't do anything that'll—"

"Cause a problem," she completed, wishing she could
kiss him instead of just expressing her gratitude with a smile.
She hadn't let herself acknowledge it before, fearing it was
only because she wanted it so much that she was letting
herself see something that wasn't there. But now, though he
looked far more reluctant than willing, he'd just agreed to
her request on nothing more than his faith in her.

"I promise," she whispered when what she really wanted to say was *I love you*. She knew she couldn't do that. Not yet. The bond growing between them was still too fragile, too new to withstand that test.

"Two minutes," Matt confirmed. Smiling at her, he shook his head and nudged her out to the sidewalk. "I can't believe I'm actually going to do this."

Eden couldn't, either, but her mind was already racing ahead. A couple of minutes. It wasn't much time, but it would be all she'd have to convince Niki that she'd never be able to find his brother if she didn't have more help. That would be the easy part. Once she had his approval, then the real battle would begin.

She had absolutely no idea how she'd do it, but somehow she had to talk Matt into helping her help Niki.

Eight

Like royalty holding court among his tuxedoed and expensively gowned subjects, Niki stood beneath one of the enormous chandeliers in the Academy of Music's elegant ballroom, sipping champagne while he smiled benignly at the two blue-haired matrons gushing their praises over his matinee performance that afternoon. Eden was right beside him, translating every flattering adjective in the English language and wishing Matt would hurry up and do something so Sergei would stop hovering around.

"Truly inspired," the larger of the two women effused, drawing attention to the profusion of rings she wore by dramatically placing her hand on the elaborate diamond necklace supported by her ample chest. "Paganini couldn't have executed those *spiccatos* and *bow tremolos* more beautifully. Tell him that, dear."

After Eden dutifully relayed what a nice job Niki had done with the bouncing strokes of his bow and the rapidly repeated short ones the woman with the rock collection referred to, Niki acknowledged the compliments with a gracious bow. With a smile that looked more pained than pleased, he then turned to Eden. "Please, *please*, get me away from these two," he implored, his voice low, even though the women obviously couldn't understand what he was saying. "Their admiration is most flattering, but enough is enough."

Sergei seemed to agree. Mumbling a rather weary "Amen" in Russian, he accepted the cup of tea he'd requested of one of the uniformed waiters.

Armed with the mini-arsenal of diplomatic excuses PR people maintained for those who insisted on monopolizing a guest of honor's time, she gave Niki's admirers a gentle smile of her own. "Mr. Dubikov is most pleased that you enjoyed his work, but he must ask that you excuse him now. He's promised to speak with..."

Between the time she'd said "excuse" and "speak" an awkward hush had fallen over the crowded room. Conversations dropped off abruptly, and the string quartet playing in the corner opposite the champagne fountain hit a few discordant notes before lapsing into silence. For a few seconds absolutely nothing could be heard but a faint scuffling noise and the low, rumbling tones of male voices.

To cover the suddenly uncomfortable atmosphere, the quartet resumed the piece they'd been playing and an instant later the room was buzzing with subdued voices as the guests began talking again. No one had moved, but every head in the place had turned toward the long bank of double doors leading to the entry foyer.

As Niki's bejeweled devotee added a few more wrinkles to her face with her scowled "Well, I never..." Eden caught sight of Ivan. Threading his way through the ocean of taffeta, lace and velvet, he came to a halt in front of Sergei.

Whatever he said was lost to Eden in the confused voices coming from around them.

"Does anyone know what happened?" someone inquired from her right.

"What do you suppose that was all about?"

"How awful," someone else muttered.

"How embarrassing," a feminine voice expanded.

"Utterly disgraceful."

"Oh, Agatha," a male voice responded. "Stop being so dramatic."

"I'm *not* being dramatic, Hubert. This was Odella's first official function as President and she's probably mortified. I certainly would be."

"I'm sure you would. You overreact to everything."

Just as Eden was thinking that everyone had developed a propensity for overreaction lately, Sergei turned to those who'd gathered at the sound of Ivan's rapid-fire Russian.

"There seems to be small problem at entrance. Not to concern yourselves. Please continue." Calmly adding to Eden that "Matt Killian asks for me," he left Ivan holding his tea.

Ivan, his mouth pinched and his eyes on Sergei's retreating back, promptly deposited the cup and saucer on a passing tray of champagne. Eden was watching Sergei, too, and trying to figure out if her heart had actually just slid up into her throat. The knot there certainly made it feel as if it had.

She'd asked Matt to find a way to divert Sergei, but she'd expected him to be a lot more discreet about it. What had he done? And how in heaven's name was he going to justify interrupting an entire reception?

Wondering if he got this same sinking feeling in the pit of his stomach whenever she did something unexpected, she swallowed her anxiety and glanced at the two men beside her. Rather than wasting precious seconds speculating about what Matt was doing, she had to make use of whatever time he could get for her. "Pardon us," she said to no one in particular and gave Niki's arm a surreptitious yank.

Niki immediately caught the message in that gesture. Ivan, preoccupied with a platter of shrimp canapés bobbing through the chattering crowd, hadn't noticed it at all. When he glanced back to Eden she gave him a quick little nod, snatched a cocktail napkin and a handful of hors d'oeuvres when they moved within reach, and slipped the paper-wrapped delicacies into his jacket pocket. A moment later the grinning guard assumed his post beside a large potted palm a discreet twenty feet away.

Three interruptions, ten minutes and a thousand frantic heartbeats later, Sergei returned. Hoping Matt's half of this little charade hadn't met with as much resistance as hers had, Eden did her best not to sound anxious. "Is everything all right?" she asked, enormously pleased with her polite tone.

"There is no problem." Squinting through his wire-rimmed glasses, Sergei glanced behind him. "We should leave here soon. Nikolai will have a meeting at hotel early in morning. He must rest." Frowning now, he adjusted his cummerbund and looked back at her. "Where is my tea?"

Telling him she'd go get him a fresh cup, Eden quickly excused herself before Sergei could say another word. She had to find Matt. And from now on, she promised herself, she wouldn't get upset with him when he got upset with her. She'd almost given herself a coronary during the past ten minutes. Poor Matt had probably been working on one ever since this tour began.

"What did you do?" she whispered when she found him leaning against the wall in the plushly carpeted and richly panelled foyer. "And why did you cause such a commotion about it?"

Matt didn't answer her right away. He allowed his gaze to wander from the high collar of her gown, over the enticing curve of her breasts, then skim lightly down to where the heavy green velvet touched the floor. The return journey was just as unhurried and every bit as thorough. He knew every square inch of her body and the way he visually stripped her left her fully aware of what his mind was seeing.

Smiling into her eyes, he calmly said, "I didn't do a thing."

"Oh, come on," she began, concern over his part in the disruption veiling the pleasure she felt at his unveiled inspection. "There isn't a single person in there who doesn't know something happened. Everybody's still talking about it."

"I wish you could hear yourself." Chuckling, he uncrossed his arms and glanced toward the small groups gathered about the lounge area. Then, deciding he should probably keep his hands to himself, he pushed them into his pockets. This time, though, he didn't go fishing around for change. "You're beginning to sound just like me. Did you talk to Niki?"

It was obvious enough that Matt wasn't going to tell her what he'd done. Giving him a nod to indicate that she had, Eden felt her pulse quicken when he focused on her mouth. "I want to talk to you."

"I want to, uh . . . 'talk' to you, too."

The husky tone of his voice washed over her, compounding the effect of his smoldering blue eyes. Her knees grew weak every time he looked at her like that and the implication in his words had her consciously locking them. "I mean *speak*," she tried to clarify. "You know—communicate?"

"I think we communicate quite well. Don't you?"

Ducking her head, she hugged her arms. "Matt, please."

"I didn't think women did that anymore." Tipping her chin up with one finger, he smiled down at her.

"Did what?"

"Blush."

"It's just warm in here," she informed him, trying to explain away the heat she could feel in her cheeks. Needing very much to change the subject before his little half smile could wreak more havoc on her nerves, she pulled his hand away. Pushing back the cuff of his white shirt and dark-gray suit jacket, she quickly checked his watch. "Sergei said Niki's got a meeting in the morning—which," she pertly added, "I suppose you didn't have anything to do with, either. It's almost eleven, so I should get back in there and start him on his goodbyes."

"I'll have the cars out front at eleven-thirty. That will put us back at the hotel a little before twelve."

"Perfect."

Pushing his hands back in his pockets to keep from pulling her to him, he chuckled. "Why perfect?"

"Because then you can meet me at midnight in the lounge and—"

"The lounge?" he cut in, doing a terrible job of hiding the disappointment flickering across his expression.

"The lounge," she repeated firmly, feeling his eyes on her bare back as she turned to walk away. That wasn't where Matt wanted to meet her and she knew it.

"Oh, Eden," Matt called just as she took her third step. "Have Androvich explain about what happened a while ago." Quite serious now, he reverted to his usual brusque professionalism. "I didn't have to do anything. Some kid showed up with his suitcases wanting to be hired on as Niki's servant in exchange for violin lessons. He can give you the details. I've got something else I want to discuss with you."

Not particularly crazy about the way he'd delivered that last statement, she hurried back into the glitz and glitter to rescue Niki. Halfway through the room, she remembered to tell a waiter about Sergei's tea.

"Why did you want to meet me here?"

Eden watched Matt lower himself into the thickly upholstered chair across from her, his eyes steady on hers as he pulled the sides of his jacket together and leaned back. Turning her glance to the returning cocktail waitress, she wondered if she shouldn't have ordered something stronger than wine. False courage, she supposed, would be better than none at all. "Because I noticed that hardly anyone's ever down here this time of night. I guess they prefer the bar upstairs."

The lounge of their hotel was a spacious, sunken area filled with deep, comfortable easy chairs and sofas arranged into intimate groupings. Dimmer switches were lowered to bathe everything in twilight and the candles flickering on the tables enhanced the serene atmosphere. She wanted a sense of calm so Matt wouldn't come unglued when she finally found the nerve to ask for his help.

Feeling like the coward she was for not getting it over with, she looked over at him. "You wanted to discuss something with me?"

"Scotch," he told the waitress as she placed a wineglass in front of Eden. "Better make that a double. Yes," he muttered to Eden as the woman hurried off.

Matt didn't say another word until he'd secured his own drink, tested its strength and placed the glass on the table. Checking out the only two other people in the lounge, an elderly couple seated at the opposite end of the room, he drew a deep breath. "Eden," he began quietly, "do you trust me?"

The question was so unexpected that all she could do was stare at the blue eyes holding hers so cautiously. Of course she trusted him. Didn't she?

Her silent question caught her as off guard as Matt's had. Surprised to find herself hesitating over what she thought should have been an unequivocally affirmative answer, she quietly inquired, "Why do you ask?"

"Because if you do, then you should be able to confide in me. I'm responsible for anything that happens to Niki while he's here, and I'm sorry but I can't keep sitting back and pretending nothing's going on when I know it is. How am I supposed to keep you out of trouble if I don't know what you and Niki are up to?"

"Is that what you wanted to talk about? What Niki wants?"

Expecting resistance, Matt steeled himself for what could very well turn into a major argument. He'd kept quiet for days, but he simply couldn't do it any longer. "That's exactly what I want to talk about."

"Fine," she shocked him by saying. "Because that's what I wanted to talk to you about, too. I just hope you're not going to be as pigheaded about this as Niki was. You have no idea how hard it was to convince him to let me tell you." Taking another sip of wine, she leaned forward. "You've got to promise me something first, though."

Matt clearly looked like he wasn't going to be pushed any farther. The way he growled "Eden," made it sound as if he was willing to add only a few more seconds to his wait of several days.

"Not until you promise."

"Did anyone ever tell you you're stubborn?"

"Sure. Mom does all the time. Will you promise?"

"Maybe. What is it?"

"That you won't interrupt until I've finished, and when I'm done that you'll help me."

"Okay to the first part. No way to the last. At least," he qualified, when she frowned at him, "not until I hear what you have to say."

She supposed that was fair enough and as quickly and concisely as she could, she relayed the story of Pasha, not at all surprised to note that Matt didn't so much as raise an eyebrow at the mention of Niki's brother. In fact, he remained totally expressionless for the entire ten minutes it took her to relate the conversations she'd managed with Niki.

"Well?" she asked, wishing he'd do something other than sit there staring at his half-empty glass. "Will you help me find him? Giving Pasha news of his family can't possibly hurt anyone and it would mean the world to Niki."

"The world, huh?" Still contemplating his ice cubes, Matt mulled over everything Eden had said. But it wasn't what Niki wanted her to do that he found so compelling. It was Eden and her willingness to go to such lengths to help someone she'd probably never see again once this tour was over. If she would do that for a person who occupied only one month of her life, what kind of loyalty would she exhibit for someone who wanted more than that?

Cutting himself off before the thought could confuse his feelings about her further, he drained the last of his drink.

To Eden's utter amazement, she heard him mumble a tight "All right. All it'll take is a phone call in the morning."

One call? she thought. She'd probably caused AT&T's stock to rise three points with all the fruitless calls she'd made, and *he* only had to make one call. "All right?" she repeated in disbelief. "Just like that?"

He eyed her dully. "No, Eden. Not just like that. I thought about it and, like you said, it shouldn't hurt anything." With the uncomfortable feeling that he'd probably consider helping her even if it might, he reached for his billfold. He'd pay for the drinks now and get them out of here. No telling what he'd commit himself to if he let her keep him here drinking doubles.

He said he'd thought about it. Obviously, she decided, recalling his statement about needing to think long and hard about particular matters, some of his decisions could be reached more rapidly than others. "Matt." She leaned forward, reaching out to cover his hand with hers when he laid some bills on the table. "Thank you."

Turning his hand to curl his fingers through hers, he smiled wryly. "If you don't mind, I'll wait until after you've talked to Pasha before I tell you you're welcome." He pulled her to her feet as he rose. "No sense being premature."

"Your confidence is overwhelming," she teased, taking pleasure in the relaxed way he was holding her hand as they left the lounge. With Matt's agreement, she sensed a deepening closeness between them, a mutual dependence on each other to attain a common goal. Well, almost common, she mentally corrected as they stepped into the elevator. Her goal was to find Pasha; Matt's was to make sure she stayed out of trouble when she did. "One of these days," she said with a soft little laugh, "I might actually start to think you trust me."

She'd offered the comment lightly, but the instant she said the words, Matt turned toward her. "What makes you think I don't?"

A nicely attired, middle-aged woman darted between the doors just as they started to close. Not sparing Eden or Matt so much as a glance, she faced forward.

The list of reasons Eden could have recited in answer to his question was sacrificed in favor of a glance that clearly said, You've got to be kidding. With that steel-trap memory of his, he couldn't possibly have forgotten that he'd all but accused her of planning to sabotage the tour the day it began.

"What makes me think that?" she asked, feigning bewilderment when they left the silent woman behind in the elevator. "Gee, I don't know, Matt. Maybe it was your insistence that I always ride in the same car with you. Or," she added in teasing innocence, "before that when you so graciously informed me that I had a way of making things go wrong."

She'd thought he'd smile. Instead, when she glanced up at him, she found his expression quite sober.

"There are different levels of trust, Eden." Catching her by the shoulders when they reached her door, he turned her to face him. What she saw in the probing depths of his eyes shook her far more than his heated touch. "You forgot to answer my question."

She hadn't forgotten to answer his question any more than she'd forgotten what it was. "Do you trust me?" he'd asked back in the lounge, and she had evaded. The same hesitation she'd felt a while ago surfaced again. "On what level?"

When Matt had asked that question earlier, he hadn't realized how important her response would be. All he'd wanted was to know if she believed him enough to share a confidence. Now, suddenly, what he wanted—needed—was to know if there was a chance she might believe *in* him. "The most basic," he heard himself admit.

Unable to break the intensity of his gaze, she slowly shook her head. "I don't know."

She couldn't be assured that he wouldn't hurt her. She couldn't know that he wouldn't reject her love if he ever discovered it. She had no confidence at all in what might happen between them in the future. In two weeks, he could walk away from her and never look back. They'd never spoken of tomorrow—and tomorrows were what she wanted. "But I know I can rely on you to help me help Niki."

Her eyes. He could usually tell what she was feeling by the emotions flickering through those silver-green depths. Now, though, there was something guarded about them, a kind of protective shield that had never been there before. Knowing he was the cause of that unfamiliar wariness made him feel as if he'd just blotted out the sun. "We'll find Pasha," he assured her, wishing he knew why he felt compelled to build on the faith she did have in him.

Wanting nothing more than to erase the haunted look her soft smile didn't quite cover, he brushed his lips across her forehead. "Give me your key."

A moment later, he'd pushed the door open. Stopping her before she could cross the room to turn on one of the lamps, he drew her against him. Beneath his hands, he felt her stiffen. Letting his fingers slip from her shoulders to curve around her upper arms, he watched her head lower. The room was dark, but with the drapes open, there was enough light to let him see the protective way she hugged her arms around herself. "Eden? What's wrong?"

Nothing. Everything, she thought, slowly stepping back. "I don't know," she lied, fully aware that she was already hurting. It made no sense at all. He was here. He wanted her. She wanted him. Yet, the thought of losing him had her pulling away. It wasn't like her to assume that something would go wrong before it did. But that's exactly what she was doing and she couldn't seem to help it. Had Matt become such a part of her that she was beginning to think the way he did?

Matt watched her move past the shadowy outlines of the room's furnishings to the window, her attention on the lights reflecting off the river. Following silently, he paused at the chair beside the dresser to remove his jacket. With an absent shrug, he slipped the straps of his shoulder holster down his arms, dropping the leather-encased gun into the chair. Eden had never said a word about his need to carry the firearm, but more than once he'd seen her flinch when she'd put her arms around him and come in contact with it. She didn't care for guns. That was obvious. But she seemed to accept their necessity.

"I wonder where they're all going," he heard her say as he took another step toward her. Her voice was hushed, her delicate features pensive as she contemplated the late-night traffic. It wound toward the turnpike, ribbons of white and red lights weaving through the black and gray cityscape as individual drivers raced toward their destinations. "I wonder," she began again, "where we're going."

Eden closed her eyes, waiting for the moment when she would sense Matt's withdrawal. She really wasn't trying to press him. She just didn't see any point in self-delusion. Better to know where I stand, she thought, than find out later...

The feel of Matt's arm around her shoulders, of him drawing her back against him to rest his chin on her head, effectively prevented any further perfection of her new-found pessimism.

"So that's it," he said, his sigh causing the fine wool of his vest to move slightly against her bare back. "You know, honey, if you were anyone else, I'd be pulling a disappearing act right about now."

Blinking at the lights she was no longer really seeing, she refused to let her hope surface again. "You would?"

"Mmm." With that illuminating response, he brought his lips to the scented skin behind her ear.

"Why?"

"Because I won't lie my way into someone's bed." The tip of his tongue traced along her earlobe, the warmth of his breath causing a reactive shiver to skitter down her neck. "Because it's easier to end a relationship that can't go anywhere before feelings get involved." He pulled back a little, moving his mouth to her nape. "But with you, it's not quite that simple."

"It's not?" The question was little more than a strained whisper, a perfect reflection of the conflicting tensions his words and his touch elicited.

He loosened his arms, leaving one across her collarbone while his other hand lowered to her waist. His fingers sneaked under the low back of her gown to curve at her side. "No." Turning her then, he pulled her sharply against him. "You see, Eden, I think I need you. And that," he added, his voice heavy, "scares the hell out of me."

His last words were spoken against her lips, the need he professed manifesting itself in an incredibly sensual demand. Within seconds, though, that demand became something totally foreign; nearly frightening in its intensity.

She felt his mouth grow hard, his tongue insistent as it pushed past her lips. The taste of him created a chain reaction of sensations, but the pressure of his mouth was almost painful. There was a savage quality in the way he sought her, a certain angry domination in the bold thrusts of his tongue. His passion was raw, an alien form of the desire she'd come to know.

She was crushed against him, the muscled strength of his arms holding her captive to the devastating assault. She tried to lift her hands—whether to touch him or push him away, she didn't know—but he had her pinned too tightly for her to free them from her sides. So much tension coiled his body that she felt as if she were wrapped in bands of iron. It was only when he impatiently unhooked the collar of her gown's halter and pulled the top to her waist that she could move at all. Her hands rose to his shoulders as he greedily cupped her breast, his mouth still working feverishly against hers. She felt herself drowning in a sea of confused sensations.

This was completely unlike the sweetly tender explorations they had shared before. There was none of the gentleness that had permeated their lovemaking. He said he thought he needed her and, had even admitted how much that frightened him. She'd heard the fear in his words. Now, as he stripped her gown past her hips, his hands rough on her sensitized skin, it was as if he were trying to exorcise that weakness, attempting to prove to himself that he could take her physically and be rid of that demon need so it couldn't threaten him any further.

Before Eden could react, Matt had taken them one step toward the bed. Then, after one ragged breath, he stood perfectly still.

"My God. What am I doing?" With his hand pressed to the base of her spine, he stared down at her. In the darkness, his face was shadowed. Still, what she couldn't see, she could hear: the remorse filling his every word. "Eden, I never meant..."

"Don't," she whispered, placing a finger to his lips. Shaking, she lowered her hand to his chest. The heavy thud of his heart was as rapid as her own. "Please...just hold me?"

The tiny plea was his undoing. He reached for her. Only this time, he was very careful, his touch purposefully cautious as he folded her into his arms. When she lifted her mouth to his and he felt the willingness in her kiss-swollen lips, he thought he might die from the sheer agony of wanting.

The buttons of his vest and shirt gave way as her trembling fingers worked them free. She wanted to touch him, assure him that she felt no fear over what had happened moments ago. She understood what had driven him. His need for her threatened the control he felt compelled to maintain for himself, and in trying to assert that control, he'd actually lost more than he'd gained. Maybe, just maybe, he'd find he couldn't be rid of that need so easily. Maybe, she thought, feeling him shudder when she slipped his shirt off him and pressed herself to his bared chest, that need would grow.

She pulled him with her to the bed, and soon thought was sacrificed to sensations: the feel of heated touch against heated skin when the remaining barriers of clothing were stripped away; hot kisses and the faint taste of liquor in his mouth; cool sheets and the warmth of their breath. The mingling scents of the perfume she wore and the spiciness of his soap. And the feel of him. Always the feel of his body responding to the honest passion within her.

There were no words to mar the sounds of their breathing, nothing to be said that couldn't be felt in the caresses they shared. The needs they communicated to each other were understood and reciprocated. And when he finally settled his weight over her, his hands drifting down to align them more intimately, her need for him flared with impatience—an impatience fueled by the deepest and most precious of emotions.

Awareness narrowed, funnelling into a thin stream of consciousness that acknowledged nothing but the oneness they created. She clung to him, her fingers digging into the smooth skin of his back, her face buried in the damp curve of his neck. *"Je t'aime,"* she softly declared, and lost in the sensual fog enveloping her as their passion exploded, she forgot that he could understand.

Matt heard the phrase from a long way off, the melodious sound of it nearly extinguished by the pounding of his heart. *I love you.* The words careened through his mind, adding a jolting dimension to their physical joining. He didn't acknowledge what she'd said, but later, when his heartbeat had calmed and he was quietly stroking her hair in the afterglow, he was amazed to discover that he didn't feel like running from it, either.

"He gave you a letter?" Matt followed Eden through the lobby of San Francisco's Mark Hopkins Hotel, frowning at her back as the doorman facilitated their exit and she stopped outside to hail one of the cabs parked along the curving drive. Niki was resting before his performance that night and, since Eden's services weren't needed at the moment, she'd decided to go see Pasha now. "When?"

Turning when she saw the first cab start toward her, she glanced up at Matt. He looked wonderful to her, as he always did, but far too concerned. "Before we left Los Angeles yesterday. He gave it to me during lunch."

"Androvich let him do that?"

"Sergei was in the bathroom."

"Do you know what's in it?"

Straight-faced, she shrugged. "I've never been in it but I suppose there's the usual assortment of washbasins and..."

"The letter," he growled, refusing to smile. "Do you know what's in the letter?"

"I didn't read it, if that's what you mean. It's personal. But," she went on, realizing Matt's stake in the situation, "he said I could read it to you, if you thought it was necessary." Fishing around in the side pocket of her purse, she withdrew the unsealed letter Niki had written on the Houston hotel's stationery. Eden was certain he'd prepared it while Sergei was asleep. "It's not necessary, is it?"

Matt eyed the envelope, his eyes narrowing on the Cyrillic characters Niki had printed. Seeing his hesitation, Eden withdrew the two pages inside. "I guess not," he replied, apparently feeling that Niki wasn't indulging in espionage if he hadn't even bothered to glue the thing closed. "You'd better get going."

"Right. I'll see you at the symphony hall in a couple of hours. You sure you can't sit with me?"

Only once had Matt sat with her during one of Niki's performances—and then only because she'd managed to trade her tickets with a couple stuck in the back of the hall. All of the tickets Barbara had secured for her for the various concerts were for seats at the end of either the first or second row and there were always two in case Eden wanted to invite someone. Since Eden had to get backstage during intermissions it was a very practical arrangement—just as it was practical for Matt and the rest of the agents to locate themselves in back.

"Not this time," he declined, instinct telling him he'd be better off without the distraction of her presence tonight. Resting his hands lightly on her shoulders, he pulled her forward. "I'll buy you a drink afterward."

There was more than the promise of a drink in the softly seductive kiss. Eden, predictably, felt her knees turn to liquid. It was always like that with him; always that sweet, slow invasion of senses that filled her with a hopeful longing that grew stronger with each passing day. He hadn't heard the words she'd whispered over a week ago. She was certain of that.

Hugging her arms over her suit jacket to fight the shiver that had nothing to do with the cool, damp air rolling in from the foggy bay, she let him set her back and open the door of the cab. The cabbie hadn't moved from behind the wheel. Either he was incredibly sensitive to what was happening outside his door or just plain lazy.

"Eden." Glancing up as she slid onto the cracked plastic seat, she saw that familiar look of caution in Matt's hooded blue eyes. He said nothing else. He didn't have to.

"Don't worry." Shaking her head, she pushed back the wheat-colored strands the breeze lifted across her face. "I'll just give him the letter, tell him Niki looks terrific and be back before you know it. Everything's fine."

Matt smiled into her eyes, letting the gentle light in them wash away the dreary feel of the weather. Long after the cab pulled out, he stood there with his hands jammed in his pockets worrying a nickel and fervently wishing he could believe in that confident optimism of hers.

"Oh, come on," he muttered to himself as the clouds opened to chase him back inside. All she had to do was deliver a letter. What could possibly happen to mess that up?

Nine

Naturalization papers. A public record of legal name change. A social security number corresponding with tax returns, which led to a place of employment and residence address. Eden had never realized how easy it was to find a person if you had the proper connections.

Matt, with his top-level security clearance, had those connections—along with more patience than Eden had exhibited when she'd discovered that his phone call hadn't resulted in an immediate answer. But she really hadn't minded the lecture he'd given her about the pitfalls of impatience—especially when, later that night in her room, he'd proceeded to thoroughly contradict every word he'd said when his need for her took precedence.

Her skin heating with that memory, she forced herself not to smile. Recalling the path that had led her to Niki's brother had succeeded only in leading her straight back to thoughts of Matt's lovemaking, something she had no business thinking about at the moment—not when she should be concentrating on the two people with her in this rattletrap of a cab.

"It's too dark to see it now, but coming up on the right is the moorage where Paul and I keep our boat. It's nothing fancy, but we take it out every weekend when the weather's good. Which," Mary Douglas added, turning from Eden to her husband, "isn't very often this time of year. Is it, Paul?"

Paul Douglas, also known as Pasha Dubikov, finally looked from the filmy window of the taxi to the petite, auburn-haired woman sitting between him and Eden. The same cab that had transported Eden to their home in the comfortable, middle-class suburb of San Mateo was now on its way back into San Francisco, taking them to the symphony hall and the brother Paul hadn't seen in thirty years.

"Not as often as we'd like," he said, the faintest trace of an accent in his voice. "Too much fog." A moment later, patting his wife's hand, he absently turned back to watch the street lamps flash by in the rain.

Paul's wife seemed to share Eden's talent for being able to carry on a nonstop, in-depth and personal conversation with a virtual stranger. Mary had been chattering away ever since they'd left the house. They'd just passed the high school where Paul taught math and, a few blocks before, they'd seen the library where Mary had gone to work last year after the younger of their two sons had left for college. Eden wasn't sure if the woman was pointing out the sites because she thought Eden would want to tell Niki about them, or if she was just trying to alleviate her husband's nervousness. As preoccupied as Paul seemed, Eden strongly suspected the latter.

Paul, as he'd asked her to call him, bore little resemblance to his younger brother. Of average height and build, and with a thatch of iron-gray hair that clearly betrayed his nearly fifty years, the only familial trait he seemed to share with Niki was the intelligent brown eyes behind his tortoise shell glasses.

Taking those glasses off, he slowly polished each lens. His wife, apparently recognizing something in that gesture, fell silent. A moment later Paul was voicing the thoughts that had kept him so still.

"I wasn't going to do this, Eden," he began, "and I wouldn't be going with you now if you hadn't told me how much trouble Niki had gone to to have you find me. I'd never hoped to hear from him." He replaced his glasses, the motion revealing a slight tremor in his hands. "Ever since we heard about his tour, Mary's tried to talk me into going to one of his concerts. She couldn't understand why I didn't want to. You see, I've hurt my family enough already." Cutting himself off, he cleared his throat.

"I knew as soon as you read his letter that you'd go." Mary spoke softly, her words filled with the understanding developed over twenty-two years of marriage. "You've missed him too much to stay away."

Paul said nothing. He simply tightened his grip on his wife's hand.

Turning to Eden, Mary smiled warmly. "I'll never be able to thank you enough for getting us in tonight." Then, wanting to dispel the somber mood she said, "Are you sure giving us your seats isn't an inconvenience?"

To cover the odd little lump she'd felt in her throat when she saw the emotion in Mary's hazel eyes, Eden gave a soft, dismissive laugh. "I'll just stay back in the wings. That'll save me the embarrassment of having to slip out while the orchestra's still playing before intermission. I always feel as if everybody's frowning at me when I do that."

"I just hope this doesn't cause any trouble for him," Paul said to the rain drops sheeting down the window.

Puzzled, Eden leaned forward. "Why would it?"

Eden had been ready to leave when she'd remembered the tickets in her purse. Paul had hesitated when she'd offered them, and despite the fact that he'd accepted them after she'd told him how much it would mean to Niki to know he was hearing his music, he apparently still had his doubts about attending the performance.

"There are many reasons," he informed her. "The most important is that the people with my brother consider me a traitor. There is nothing they can do to me. But the penalty for associating with a traitor is severe."

"You're his brother," Eden pointed out, frustrated that political precepts could be regarded as more important than familial ties. As far as she was concerned, nothing was stronger than family.

"They can't keep you from seeing a performance," his wife said quietly.

"No." He kept his eyes straight ahead, the slap of the windshield wipers punctuating the momentary lull between his words. "They can't. All I want to do now is hear his music. I won't even think of trying to speak to him. He won't even know I'm there."

"Yes, he will," Eden gently refuted.

An understanding silence fell over the three passengers as the cabbie accelerated down the exit ramp.

Matt didn't have any change. He'd spent his last quarter, four dimes and a nickel on an overpriced candy bar he'd bought at the hotel's gift shop. The only things in his pocket were a paper clip and a set of keys. The paper clip was being worn out between his thumb and index finger. The carpet on the floor of the mezzanine wasn't faring much better.

Slipping through the balcony door just as the orchestra began its last piece of the evening, he endured several reproachful glares as he moved silently toward the last row. "I'm going backstage," he whispered to Dom when he found him standing against the wall. "See you back there in a few minutes."

They normally didn't leave their posts until the first set of curtain calls. Sensing Matt's unease, Dom didn't point out the break in routine. Instead, he glanced down at the way Matt's hand was jammed in his pocket then back to the bunched muscle in his jaw. "Something the matter?"

"Shhh!"

"Please!" came another quiet, though equally insistent request for silence.

Lowering his voice to the point where he did little more than mouth the words, Matt muttered, "I don't know yet," and turned to scan the main floor below. A moment later, the vague feeling of uncertainty he'd been experiencing all evening compounded itself.

Eden wasn't where she was supposed to be. He knew she'd returned from her visit to Niki's brother because Steve had seen her backstage talking to Niki just before the performance began. Matt had seen her back there himself when he'd gone down to talk to her during the intermission. Because she'd been busy translating for the conductor, there'd been no opportunity to speak with her then. Now, he could see that she hadn't taken her usual place in the audience when the performance had resumed. The seats she'd been assigned were occupied, though.

Working his way back to the mezzanine, he found himself hoping that the man sitting next to the woman at the end of the first row wasn't who he thought he was. That hope wasn't an easy thing to hang on to, but for Eden, he'd do his level best not to jump to conclusions.

The thunderous applause at the end of the concert had called Niki back to the stage for his third bow by the time

Matt found Eden standing among the extra chairs and music stands cluttering the wings. With an acknowledging nod to Sergei who stood several feet behind her, he moved briskly to her side.

Tipping his head, the warm, unnervingly sexy fragrance she wore filling his nostrils, he spoke in a husky undertone. "Who are those people in your seats?"

He had his answer before she said a word. She looked up at him, her eyes shimmering in the dim light. It was apparent enough she didn't see the need for explanations, lost as she was in whatever thoughts had given her that misty, faraway look. "Niki knew he was here before I even told him," she said wistfully, then seemed a little confused when her name was called from the stage.

Seeing the conductor motioning to her, Eden swallowed the lump that had been building in her throat ever since she'd confirmed Paul's presence to Niki during the intermission. That knot settled in her stomach. Matt hadn't looked as calm as he'd sounded, the slight twitch of the muscle in his jaw indicating something other than the sense of satisfaction she felt at having brought the two brothers this close. She'd been hoping Matt would join her so they could share their accomplishment together, but he didn't seem anywhere near as touched by the reunion as she was.

Not sure if she was simply witnessing his usual reserve or if something more worrisome lurked behind his guarded blue eyes, she told him she'd be right back and moved forward, expecting to be met just out of sight of the packed house.

It didn't occur to her that her presence was actually wanted onstage. At least it didn't until Niki walked over to her, offered his arm, whispered, "You will please announce something for me?" and nudged her out under the lights. Behind her she heard the shuffle of feet as Matt and

Sergei ventured as close as they dared before they, too, could be exposed to the murmuring audience.

The members of the orchestra lowered their instruments, anticipating an announcement of the encore while thirty seconds of quick and quiet conversation took place at the podium. Then, with a bow from the conductor, Eden took the microphone to translate Niki's words to the hundreds waiting to hear them.

"The piece Mr. Dubikov wishes to play for you is a simple one," she began, her ear tuned to what Niki was saying to her even as she spoke. "It is an old song his mother...sang to him and his brother when they were young children. It begins by describing the stars in the evening sky of the Ural Mountains...and ends with a supplication for the child in the song to reach for those stars and free himself from his mother's arms. He can no longer...no longer," she repeated, willing her voice to maintain its strength, "...remember all the words, but the melody has stayed with him...as has the love of those in his memories. There is one among you who shares that affection. This," she concluded when Niki positioned himself in his chair, "is for you."

The man in the second seat at the end of the first row kept his eyes riveted on the barrel-chested violinist. Eden, her vision blurring when she saw Paul reach for his wife's hand, gracefully left the stage as Niki raised his bow.

The melody began with a haunting refrain, the slow, sweet sounds of it filling the air with bittersweet longing. From behind her, she heard Sergei gasp and glancing toward him, saw shock replaced by the grim set of his mouth.

"This song is forbidden in our country," he announced to both Matt and Eden, though he didn't take his eyes from the man onstage.

The music seemed to reach beyond the walls, the sheer beauty of it defying any boundary or restraint. That was why Sergei's words seemed so implausible. How could anything so lovely be forbidden anywhere? Before she could think better of it, she heard herself say, "This isn't your country," and drew a shaky breath.

A split second later, Matt's sharply muttered "Eden!" let her know what a nice job she'd just done of putting her diplomatic foot in her mouth.

"Well, it's not," she whispered at him over her shoulder. "He can play anything he wants to here."

"For whom is he playing?" The small man with the forbidding voice turned to her, his arms crossed and his expression as unforgiving as he could make it. "Who is this 'one among you' to whom he refers?"

Eden could feel Matt's eyes boring down on the back of her head. Preferring Sergei's glower to the displeasure she knew she'd find in Matt's glare, she took Sergei by the arm and pulled him back toward the exit.

They came to a halt beside the technician working the complex assortment of electronic lighting equipment. Ignoring the young woman's presence, Eden quickly apologized to Sergei for her lapse in discretion and abandoned defiance in favor of pleading. Sergei was not an unreasonable man. He was a bit like Matt since he followed the instructions he'd been given to the letter, but he could listen to reason—at least she hoped so.

"Mr. Androvich," she began, all but ignoring Matt when he came up beside her. One slightly defensive male was all she could deal with at the moment. "The 'you' is Niki's brother. But . . ."

"Pasha Petrovich Dubikov is traitor," Sergei intoned flatly.

Traitors were people like Judas and Benedict Arnold. Not quiet, unassuming math teachers. "You remember that kid who crashed Niki's reception in Philadelphia? The one who wanted to go to Moscow with Niki so he could study under him?"

Sergei nodded, adjusted his glasses, and recrossed his arms.

Encouraged by the fact that he was listening, Eden plunged in. She'd either sink or swim, but she wouldn't flounder. "Did you think of him as a traitor?"

"Of course not."

"No," Eden agreed, her voice remarkably calm. "You didn't. You felt sorry for him. Even though he didn't have enough talent to study under a master, you pitied him because he wanted something he couldn't have. It was like that with Paul... er, Pasha," she corrected, very aware of the tension radiating from Matt. "He was looking for something he couldn't find in his own country, a way to have what he felt he needed. You didn't look on that American boy as a traitor to political beliefs. You saw him as a young man who was willing to do anything to have what he wanted. Can't you see Pasha like that?"

An unexpected, but very welcome look of consideration passed over Sergei's pinched features. "I cannot let my personal feelings interfere."

"Interfere with what?" she quietly pleaded.

"His duty," Matt supplied in a voice as taut as the strings on Niki's bow. "We all have rules to follow, Eden."

The way he stressed that "all" was a clear reminder that she had rules to follow, too—the ones she was breaking right now by stepping on some very sensitive political toes.

"Thank you," Sergei said, his attention darting straight back to Eden. Something that could have passed for regret flashed through his bespectacled glance. "You are sentimental, Eden Michaels, and because you are a woman that is excused. Nikolai knew when he came to your country that he would not be allowed to communicate with his brother.''

"Niki has said all he can through his music, Eden," Matt added, sensitivity vying with the warning in his eyes. "That will have to be enough."

His brow furrowed at the sudden quiet filling the wings. The last strains of Niki's melody had faded and nothing but absolute silence could be heard as the three of them moved together toward the black curtain beside the stage. Then the entire place erupted with the thunder of applause as the audience rose to their feet, the orchestra joining them in the cacophony that followed Niki into the wings.

"We will go now," Niki said, handing his bow and violin to Sergei. "Please."

Sergei nodded, following his charge with a quiet "I will join you with vodka at the hotel."

Matt frowned at Eden. Keeping his eyes on her, though she avoided his, he decided that now was not the time to ask her just what in the hell she thought she'd accomplish by bringing Pasha back with her. There were a few other things he wanted to say, but those, too, could wait. "What did they say?"

"Niki wants to leave. Sergei wants a drink," she repeated, risking a glance around the curtain. The audience was still on their feet, their applause an entreaty for the master to return. Just beyond the curtain, she caught a glimpse of Paul and Mary as they hurried out.

First thing in the morning, she told herself, she'd call Mary and see how Paul was doing. Maybe, just maybe, none of this had been such a hot idea after all.

It was easy to see Matt didn't think so, but since he said nothing other than "We'd better go," it was hard to tell how he really felt.

Matt wished he knew what it was he did feel. Telling himself he was displeased with Eden only on a professional basis wasn't working at all. It wasn't simple displeasure that had tied his stomach in knots. Nor was it that predictable unpredictability he'd come to expect from her. The sensation in his gut was almost like fright, but had nothing at all to do with the fear of what could have happened had Androvich been a little less understanding of Eden's naïveté.

Ever since Dom had asked him what he was going to do about Eden, it seemed that Matt could think of little else. For days, he'd felt as if he were hanging on the edge of something, not at all sure if he should tighten his grip or simply let go and see what caught him at the bottom. That disconcerting sensation of losing control clouded his thinking, making it nearly impossible for him to divorce his emotions from professional judgments.

Quite probably, he told himself, he should turn around and leave. It would probably be better to wait until tomorrow to talk to her.

"Why couldn't you have left well enough alone?" he asked, from where he stood by the window in Eden's room. "And what," he went on, disbelief the only feeling he allowed himself to show, "ever possessed you to talk to Androvich like that?"

All the time Eden had been talking to Niki's manager, Matt had been torn between wanting to shut her up and outright admiration for her nerve. Now, he was caught between wanting to take her in his arms or shake some sense into that beautiful head of hers.

"I guess I was just frustrated with the stupidity of all this." She dropped her wool coat onto the chair beside him. A moment later, she took her shoes off. "Niki and Pasha are brothers," she added, as if that should explain everything.

Eden would have given anything to understand Matt's puzzling mood. The way his jaw was working indicated irritation. Yet, in the limo, he'd shown nothing but patience while she'd told him how Paul and Mary had come to join her. Needing him to be receptive, she curled her fingers over his arm. He immediately backed away.

"All right," Matt conceded, refusing to let himself respond to the flash of uncertainty in her eyes when she, too, stepped back. "So they're brothers. I feel just as bad as you do about their circumstances, but there's nothing we can do about that. The issue here is what you did. Rather," he corrected, raking his fingers through the silvering strands of his dark hair, "what you failed to do. Didn't you stop to consider what could have happened if Androvich hadn't been willing to dismiss what you did as an act of sentimentality? What if he'd decided that, in your official capacity, you were deliberately defying his government?"

Eden paled. "I hadn't thought about that."

"I'm sure you didn't. You never stop to think about anything until it's too late. Half the time I'm not even sure you think about it then."

Matt knew he shouldn't have said that—even though, at the moment, it certainly seemed like an unquestionable truth. Why in the hell, he thought, hadn't he followed his instincts a few moments ago and left before any of this got started?

Eden tilted her chin, Matt's accusation adding yet another emotion to the confounding variety she'd experienced in the past few hours. But the sympathy, satisfaction, disappointment and frustration she felt for Niki and his brother were forgotten as the defensiveness Matt elicited took over. "That is not true."

"The hell it's not! Damn it, Eden!" he yelled, as frustrated with himself as he was with her. "You told me all you were going to do was deliver a letter! I trusted you, and look at what you did."

He might as well have slapped her. What little color was left in her cheeks drained below the bow of her blue blouse. Turning her stricken look to the floor, she quietly studied the nap in the beige carpet. While she had to admit she'd done a bit more than deliver Niki's letter by encouraging Paul to attend tonight's performance, she refused to accept full responsibility for what had happened.

"Now you feel I've betrayed that trust because things changed a little." Her voice flat to hide the hurt, she narrowed her eyes in challenge. "Hasn't it occurred to you that Paul and Niki had a part in this? That Paul wanted to see his brother and that Niki would have played that piece whether I'd introduced it or not?"

"You introducing it doesn't have anything—"

"You're sure making it sound that way," she cut in, feeling herself take another plunge on the emotional roller coaster she'd been riding all evening. There seemed to be very little room for error in that trust of his.

"I didn't mean you were responsible for that."

"Then what *do* you mean?" she shot back, wishing she could be rid of the feeling that he was angry about something other than what they were yelling about. "We're not communicating, Matt. What I'm hearing is that you think I'm to blame for what happened tonight. And I'm trying to tell you that while things could have gotten worse, they didn't!"

"And I'm trying to tell *you* that I'm not so sure I can go through the rest of my life holding my breath!"

"Who's asking you to?" she demanded and, a full second later, felt the delayed impact of his angry words. Her own fury gave way to horror when she realized what she'd said in return.

The rest of my life. The phrase echoed inside her head, Matt's muttered "Beats the hell out of me," barely audible as he stormed across her room.

Her voice was considerably quieter than it had been moments ago. "Where are you going?"

"What difference does it make?"

"It doesn't! I mean it does..."

Leaving his hand on the knob when he reached the door, he jerked around. Until he'd heard himself say it out loud, he hadn't realized how much he'd been dwelling on the kind of commitment he knew she wanted. Having finally pegged the reason for his unsettled state, he'd immediately taken to his heels. Hardly an honorable path, but it was the only one that didn't lead straight to the bottom of that unknown void he'd been struggling against. He needed some space and some time. Definitely, time.

"You got it right when you said we weren't communicating, Eden. But I do understand that this doesn't have anything to do with Niki or his brother. It's strictly us. The way I feel right now, I'm not so sure anything I say will make any sense." Drawing his fingers through his hair, the gesture having become somewhat of habit lately, he muttered a profound imprecation that would have been understood in any language and pulled the door open. "I'm so damned confused I don't even know what's going on anymore."

She could certainly identify with that. It wasn't at all unusual for them to argue, but always before she'd known what they were arguing about. The lines of communication had not only broken down, but from the looks of things, they were in danger of severing completely.

Reaching his side before he could step into the hall, she curled her fingers around his wrist. "Matt, I'm sorry." She didn't quite know what she was apologizing for, or what it was in his expression that made her lower her hand. She only knew that something had gone terribly wrong and, somehow, it was her fault.

Eden held her breath when she saw the hesitation etched in his chiseled features. Matt was not a man to be pushed. She knew that well enough, yet it took every ounce of self-discipline she had not to tell him how desperately she loved him, how much it hurt to have him so upset with her. Or maybe, she thought, her heart pounding frantically, it was the instinct for self-preservation that made her hold her tongue. She had the horrible feeling that what he was going to say was something she didn't want to hear.

That feeling was confirmed by the anguish entering Matt's eyes when he finally looked down at her. "You don't have to be sorry," he said, willing himself to back away. God help him, he didn't want to hurt her. "I know you were only trying to help Niki. It's just . . ." Fully aware of the pain in her eyes, hating himself for having put it there, he offered the only explanation he could that might make her understand why he was doing this to them. "We've been together for the last twenty-four days, Eden. Together every night for over a week. Sometimes a little distance helps put things in perspective. I need that distance right now."

A moment later he was walking away, Eden turning back into her room before the desperation she felt could make her run after him. There was nothing she could say that would make any difference. For one heart-stopping moment he'd looked like a cornered animal, the fright in his eyes as visible as his fierce desire to escape. She'd never meant to make him feel that way. She'd tried so hard to give him the room she knew he needed.

Tomorrow, she promised herself, willing the moisture in her eyes to go away. It would be better tomorrow.

* * *

It was worse. Matt didn't ignore her, but she almost wished he would. His attitude was every bit as polite and remote as it had been in Italy, only now that indifference cut through her as bitterly as the icy wind that greeted their arrival in Portland. She wasn't the only one who noticed the change. Dom had asked her if something was wrong just before they boarded the plane, telling her that Matt had practically bitten his head off that morning when he'd asked if everything had been straightened out with Androvich. That matter had, but Matt made no effort to get her alone and explain his sudden and complete withdrawal.

By the time the tour ended five days later, no explanation was necessary. Eden clearly understood the unspoken message in their short and guarded conversations. He'd once told her that it was better to get out of a relationship before feelings got involved. If his coolness was any indication, it was clear enough that he'd escaped unscathed. It was too bad she hadn't. She loved him—and it was over.

Numb. Eden had felt that way ever since she, Dom, Steve and Matt had landed in Washington, D.C., after seeing Niki off in Boston. Sergei, Ivan and Boris had marked their departure with polite goodbyes. Niki had kissed both her cheeks, then wrapped her in a huge bear hug before telling her he would never forget his beautiful American friend. Even Dom and Steve had made a point of telling her to keep in touch when they'd piled out of the cab in front of the State Department building Monday afternoon. Matt had said nothing. He'd simply held her eyes for three very long seconds, then lowered his head and walked away.

"You want to fight the mob in the cafeteria or brave the rain and go to Katz's Deli for lunch?" Barbara Yu stood in the middle of Eden's cluttered office, her eyes on the paper clip Eden was unfolding. "It's time to eat, Eden."

"You go ahead," Eden returned, hoping her smile didn't look as plastic as it felt. "I've got to finish translating this letter for Harry." Dropping the clip next to several others on the file beside her, she reached for the sheets of paper she'd been staring at for the better part of an hour. The correspondence was simple enough. It was just that her concentration was shot and she kept having to look up the Spanish equivalents she knew she knew but couldn't think straight enough to recall. It had been like this all week.

"Food, Eden," Barbara said gently. "It's basic to human survival. Suicide by starvation isn't going to solve a darn thing."

"I'm not contemplating anything that drastic. I'm just not hungry."

The door closed, Barb's sympathy dissolving to the sternness she usually reserved for her dealings with the kids from the mail room. "Listen up here. I know it's rough. The rat dumped you. But it's not the end—"

"His name's Matt," Eden interrupted quietly.

"...of the world," Barb went on without acknowledging the minor correction. "The only reaction I've seen from you since you got back is when the phone rings, and then you jump and stare at the thing as if it was too hot to touch. Other than that, you're acting like a zombie. Frankly," she pointed out, "you don't look much better."

"Maybe I should switch my brand of makeup."

Exasperated, Barb threw up her hands. "Maybe you should call the creep and unload some of that pain you're carrying. Catharsis is good for the soul, you know."

"I can't do that."

"No," her friend agreed. "You probably couldn't. But I know I'd feel better if it were me and I could get in the parting shot." The lovely woman softened her tone. "Don't you want to talk to him before he leaves?" At the quizzical frown passing over Eden's face, she quietly added, "He put in for a transfer the day after you got back."

For one completely miserable instant, the numbness subsided enough to let the hurt through again. Crossing her arms protectively over the white buttons on her black sheath, Eden stiffened. "It's nice to know the inter-bureau secretarial grapevine still works. Where's he going?" she heard herself ask, not really sure she wanted to know.

"He's asked for Austria. Betty said a security slot just opened."

They spoke German in Austria, a language Matt knew she had yet to master. She'd told him that to become proficient in German, she'd probably have to spend a lot of time listening to it being spoken—something she couldn't afford to do without working, and something her work wouldn't allow her to do because the department wouldn't waste its time training her when she already had skills it could use.

Obviously, Matt had picked a place where he wouldn't be in danger of running into her. "I hope he'll be happy there."

"You're unbelievable." Hands on her hips, Barb shook her head in utter disbelief. "You actually sound like you mean that."

Eden did mean it. No matter what had happened, she still loved Matt. She'd always love him for letting her see a part of himself he'd never been able to share with anyone else. She hadn't had all of him, but she knew she'd gotten as close to him as he'd let anyone get. He'd told her that much. And because he'd never lied to her, she believed him.

"I do mean it," she said, her smile very soft. "I can't hate him, Barb. I've tried. The only thing I hate is the idea of living without him, but if he's happier without me, then that's what I want for him." The softness faded, replaced with the first real emotion that had been visible in her eyes for days: disgust. *"Madre de Dio,"* she muttered, shoving her hair behind her ears as she frowned at her dear, well-meaning friend. "Did that sound as corny as I think it did? I'm actually getting maudlin!"

Barb grinned. "No. I think you're getting better." Turning her look of approval to her watch, she pulled open the door. "Are you better enough to suffer through one of those things they euphemistically refer to as a hamburger in the cafeteria? No time for the deli now."

"Better" was a relative term. There was still plenty of room for improvement in her present mental state, and still no room in her stomach for anything but the knot that had taken up permanent residence there. "I'll pass."

"You sure?"

"Positive," Eden affirmed, knocking her pen to the floor when she firmly pushed Harry's letter to the center of her desk.

Disappointed that she hadn't accomplished her mission, Barb heaved a sigh and closed the door behind her. A moment later, just as she bent to retrieve her pen, Eden heard the door open again.

Thinking Barbara was nothing if not persistent, she kept her head down while she fished the pen from between the rollers on her chair. "I don't want to go," she repeated.

"I was afraid you'd say that. But I was sort of hoping you would at least let me ask the question first."

Eden felt her heart stop. An instant later, it made up for that missed beat by tripling its rhythm. Matt stood just inside the doorway, his expression a study in uncertainty. It was clear enough he didn't know what to expect from her.

Not feeling particularly certain herself at the moment, she slowly raised her hand to place the pen on her desk and mumbled a ridiculously polite "Come in."

The latch clicked in place, closing out the faint conversations taking place in the hallway. Eden watched him turn back to her, the little laugh lines around his eyes appearing deeper than she'd remembered. At first his silvered brown hair looked windblown, but when she saw him push his fingers through it, it was obvious that the repeated gesture had given it that casually mussed effect.

His hand fell to his side, but it didn't slip into the pocket of his dark slacks. Raising her eyes to his, she found him quietly scanning her face. He smiled faintly. "You didn't even give me a chance to ask you."

"Ask me?" she repeated as he moved to stand beside her.

"Mmm." He nodded, his glance swinging to the neat stacks of papers surrounded by the more lopsided ones on her window ledge. The leaded crystal paperweight Niki had given her as a farewell gift sat next to a half-empty cup of coffee on her desk. Half-empty, that's how he felt without her. "The question you answered when I came in," he more or less clarified. "Or were you expecting someone else?"

They still weren't communicating. Only understanding half of what he said, she drew a cautionary breath. With it came that familiar scent of soap and spice, and the forcible jolt of memories. "Barb. I thought you were Barb coming back to make me go to lunch."

She looked thinner. It had been only a week since he'd last seen her, but her cheekbones were more defined and the faint shadows beneath her guarded gray-green eyes spoke of more than a few restless nights. Had he done that to her? It was one thing for him to lose sleep, but he'd never meant to...

Touching her cheek, he cut off his mental accusations. There were more immediate matters to deal with right now. "I need to ask you something," he began, feeling some of his uncertainty ebb when her head turned to his light caress. "But I need to tell you something first. The way you first told me." Encouraged by the inquiry in her eyes, the way she looked up at him with that open vulnerability of hers, he drew a stabilizing breath. *"Je t'aime, Eden."*

I love you.

"You do?" she whispered, shocked to learn that he'd known how she felt about him all along. That sensation of disbelief, though, was nothing compared to the stunning impact of his words.

"More than I ever thought possible." Drawing his knuckles to the pulse beating frantically at her temple, he gave her that endearing half smile of his. "I think it started during the yelling match in that intersection back in Boston. But I didn't realize that's what it was until I was yelling at you about that little incident between Androvich and Niki's brother. It seems that every time I lost control of myself, a little more of you crept in."

His lips tightened then, his eyes expressing the inner turmoil that had accompanied his fight for that control. "You see, Eden," he explained, "I knew I needed you, but I didn't know how to handle that need because it was something I'd never felt before. Maybe I should have tried to talk to you about it," he said, giving voice to one of the thousand alternatives that had occurred to him during the last few sleepless nights. "Or maybe I shouldn't have worried about it so much and just accepted it."

"I don't think you could have done that."

"Probably not," he agreed, his smile returning. She knew him so well, better, it seemed at times, than he even knew himself. "But I can promise that the next time I'm upset because of you, I'll make damn sure I don't leave until things get straightened out. Not," he added, "that anything like this could happen more than once in a lifetime."

"Oh, Matt," she whispered, letting him draw her into his arms. "I love you so much."

"Thank God," he breathed and captured her lips.

The depth of his feeling was conveyed in that mind-distorting contact. He crushed her to him, giving all he'd been afraid to give her before. Eden took it, returning that physical expression of need and want and longing with the same hungry yearning she felt in him. She had no idea how long they remained locked in that soul-satisfying embrace, but when Matt finally raised his head to cup her face between his hands, the effects she felt were mirrored in his eyes.

"Can you get out of here early?" he asked, the smoky tones of his husky voice filled heavy with intent.

"Probably," she returned, sounding as shaky as she felt. "Harry said I haven't been much good to him all week, anyway."

"Harry. I think we're going to need to talk to him."

"Why?"

"Well," he began, dropping a kiss to her forehead before he pulled her head to his chest. "The question I wanted to ask you sort of affects him, too. I've put in for a transfer to Austria, honey. I want you to go with me."

"I can't get an assignment there...."

"I realize that. But with me supporting you for a while, you'd have time to work out the rough spots in your German. If you take a leave of absence, then maybe by the time a position for a translator opened up at the embassy, you could apply for it."

"You've got this all figured out, huh?"

"Yep. See any problems with it?"

"Only one."

Not liking the sound of that, he frowned down at her.

"I don't like the idea of you supporting me."

"Why not? If you're pregnant . . ."

"Pregnant!"

"That's how we get the kids," he explained patiently. "You know, those little things that grow up to be big things that need braces and . . ."

"But we're not married."

"We will be. The kids would appreciate it. Don't you think?" He hesitated, wondering if he'd gone too far too fast. "You will marry me, won't you?"

For about two seconds, she perversely entertained the thought of letting him sweat out an answer. After what he'd put her through, it was the least he deserved. "Yes," she returned in the next breath. "Oh, yes!"

She met him halfway, their kiss filled with the promise of everything they would share. It was going to be wonderful spending the rest of their lives discovering just what it was that they found so frustrating, endearing and enlightening about each other. And they'd learn. Together they'd already learned so much—a whole new form of communication. The language of love.

* * * * *

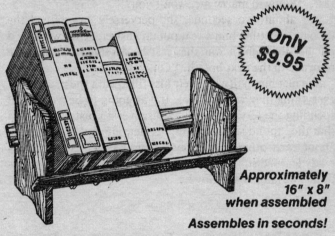

Silhouette Intimate Moments

Starting in October...

SHADOWS ON THE NILE

by

Heather Graham Pozzessere

A romantic short story in six installments from best-selling author Heather Graham Pozzessere.

The first chapter of this intriguing romance will appear in all Silhouette titles published in October. The remaining five chapters will appear, one per month, in Silhouette Intimate Moments' titles for November through March '88.

Don't miss "*Shadows on the Nile*"—a special treat, coming to you in October. Only from Silhouette Books.

Be There!

IMSS-1